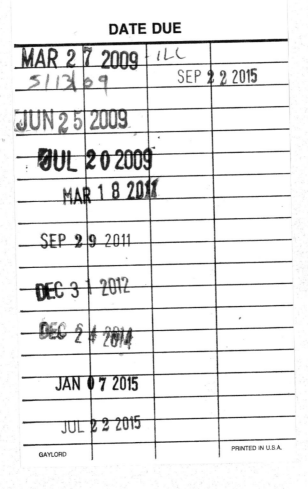

Attack of the Turtle

Attack of the Turtle

A *novel by*

Drew Carlson

Illustrations by

David A. Johnson

Eerdmans Books for Young Readers

Grand Rapids, Michigan / Cambridge, U.K.

Published 2007 by Eerdmans Books for Young Readers,
an imprint of Wm. B. Eerdmans Publishing Co.

2140 Oak Industrial Drive NE, Grand Rapids, Michigan 49505 /
P.O. Box 163, Cambridge CB3 9PU U.K.

www.eerdmans.com/youngreaders

Manufactured in the United States of America

07 08 09 10 11   7 6 5 4 3 2 1

Library of Congress Cataloging-in-Publication Data

Carlson, Drew.

Attack of the Turtle / written by Drew Carlson; illustrations by David A. Johnson.

p.   cm.

Summary: During the Revolutionary War, fourteen-year-old Nathan joins forces with
his older cousin, the inventor David Bushnell, to secretly build the first submarine
used in naval warfare.

ISBN 978-0-8028-5308-0 (alk. paper)

1. United States — History — Revolution, 1775-1783 — Naval operations — Juvenile
fiction. [1. United States — History — Revolution, 1775-1783 — Naval operations —
Fiction. 2. Submarines (Ships) — Fiction. 3. Bushnell, David, b. 1740 — Fiction.
4. Inventors — Fiction.] I. Johnson, David, 1951 Feb. 18- ill.   II. Title.

PZ7.C21649At   2006

[Fic] — dc22

2005032068

Text type set in Adobe Garamond

Display type set in Aquiline

Illustrations created with pen and ink

for Holly — D. C.

Contents

"Bushnell is a man of great mechanical powers, fertile in inventions and master of execution. . . . I then thought, and still think, that it was an effort of genius. . . ."

George Washington to Thomas Jefferson,
September 26, 1785

Chapter 1

"Wanna fight?"

Fear shot through me like a musket blast. My knees and hands started to shake.

"No, not really," I mumbled and kept walking.

Butch Hyde swaggered up beside me and leaned his face in close to mine. His breath stank, and when he spoke spittle flecked onto my cheek. *Oh Providence,* I prayed, *please open a hole in the ground and swallow me up. Get me out of this! Please.*

I looked, half hopefully, down at the dusty street. No hole had appeared.

"C'mon, Wade," Butch taunted. "You're bigger than me. Let's fight."

"Nope, not gonna," I said and turned mechanically down Main Street. Josh Laribee, my best friend, walked beside me. My uncle's farm was still five long miles away — it might as well have been in England. Butch was getting bolder and bolder. Last week he followed me halfway to the farm, taunting me, begging me to fight.

Papa sends me to Saybrook every May, saying I'll be more good to Uncle Elias on the farm than to him on the fishing boat. And every summer in Saybrook Butch torments me. Then I go the twenty miles back to New London and hear Papa growl, "What good's a son who's afraid of water?" I don't know what's worse — disappointing Papa or running from Butch.

This summer was different. When it was time to leave for Saybrook, Papa walked me to the stagecoach. "Son, you're going to be with Uncle Elias for a while. I've signed up with the Volunteers for twelve months. I'll send for you . . . when the war is over."

"Yes sir," I said, not knowing what to think.

Papa disappeared into the sea after Mama died of the fever three years ago. It was dark when he left the house and dark when he came home. Sometimes he didn't come home at all. I used to wait for him at the wharf, staring for hours at the gray sea. The other fishermen and their sons would row in, unload their catches, and go home. I'd finally go home alone and climb into bed, feeling a big, empty hole in my chest.

Now he was disappearing again — into the war.

Laughter burst from Bower's General Store. Two town boys, Morgan Fenner and John Rudd, were on the front step, enjoying the show.

"Boys, I got me a scared kitty cat coward from New London," Butch called out, walking toward the boys. "He's afraid to fight. And you know what? He's scared of water, too — just like a cat."

A fresh burst of hot shame lit my cheeks. Blood roared in my ears. I hurried on, dragging the sack of flour I'd come into town for. Josh's short legs churned beside me, trying to keep up with my long strides.

Hoots followed us down the street. "Here puss, puss, puss!" the three boys yelled, laughing. "Meow, meow! Hey pussums, how about a saucer of milk?"

As we hustled toward the edge of the village, Josh looked up into my face. His blue eyes twinkled.

"Nate, you *are* bigger than he is," he gently scolded. "You could take him, I know you could."

Josh is fourteen like me, but I'm a full foot taller. I'm six inches taller than Butch, and he's sixteen. When you're the tallest kid around, everyone thinks you shouldn't be afraid of anything.

"He'd lick me," I murmured.

"How do you know until you try?" Josh replied. "You might surprise yourself."

"Why don't you try yourself?" I shot back.

Actually, I knew Josh would stand up for himself if push came to shove. He's small, but spunky. Maybe that's why Butch and the other boys let him be.

Josh laughed. "See, Nate, even you know how to get mad."

"You're darn right I'm mad. I hope Butch gets killed by the British."

"Nate, you don't mean that. I know he's a bully, but you don't want him dead."

"Yes I do. I heard he's joining the Continentals, and I hope he never comes back from the war."

"So when is David coming home from Yale?" Josh asked. He knew when to change subjects.

"Tonight. He graduated early because of the war. He's supposed to be on the stagecoach."

Josh's house was coming up. It's on Main Street, toward the edge of town where the country begins.

I glanced back. In the distance I saw Butch, Morgan, and John in front of Bower's Store. I wondered if they were still laughing at me.

Beyond them, the village houses ran down to the wharf. Tall masts spiked the sky above the harbor. White sails breathed slowly back and forth in the soft summer breeze. Saybrook is a sea town. It sits on Long Island Sound, which flows into the Atlantic Ocean. The Connecticut coast encloses the Sound to the north. Across the water to the south, farther than you can see, is Long Island, New York.

Saybrook is also a river town. The Connecticut River flows by on the east. It's a mighty river, not like the creek-like Pochaug up by the farm. The Connecticut is a mile or more across in some places. It starts in northern New England and splits the state in two before spilling out into the Sound.

"So what is this secret project of David's?" Josh asked.

"Darned if I know," I said, shrugging. "You know David. He keeps stuff secret. His letter just said he was working on something he was real proud of but that he couldn't talk about it."

I trusted Josh not to blab, but I didn't trust him not to try to find out on his own.

What could David have invented that was so special it had to be secret? I figured it was just David being David. As long as I've known him he's been tinkering with bits of metal and building things.

Most folks around Saybrook think my cousin David is a bit odd. He's thirty-three years old, and as far as I know he's never looked at a girl, much less kissed one. He's the son of a farmer, but hates farming. When he's home he mostly sticks to himself, studying and drawing diagrams. He's a quiet, solitary sort, and smart as a whip.

All his life David wanted to go to college. We all thought he was doomed to spend his days helping his father, Nehemiah, run their little farm. A lot of families send the oldest son off to college as a kind of reward, but Nehemiah couldn't afford to let David go.

Then Nehemiah keeled over dead one day plowing the back pasture. Worked himself to death, people said. David inherited the farm and hung around working it, waiting on his mama to remarry. Aunt Sarah finally met Uncle Elias and as soon as they were married, David was off to Yale like a shot. At thirty, he was almost old enough to be the father of some of the freshmen.

That was three years ago. Now David was coming home a graduate of the class of 1776 with a secret project up his sleeve.

We reached Josh's house, and he started toward the front door. "Gotta milk the cows," he said. "Their udders will be a' aching."

Josh went inside and I headed back down the dusty street. Josh lives just two doors down from the Pratts' house. Mr. Pratt runs the Rising Sun Tavern, and he's also Saybrook's postmaster. My stomach tightened a couple notches as I passed by. Rachel Pratt is my age, and I'm always hoping to catch a glimpse of her through her bedroom window.

I think she's beautiful. All the boys do. Rachel's hair is astonishing, a thick mane of red that tumbles down over her shoulders. Her skin is as white as the swans that swim out on the river. Rachel's brown eyes sparkle and dance, and she always seems glad to see you.

I stared at the dirt as I walked by, imagining Rachel was watching me out the window, admiring me.

Suddenly the front door swung open and my heart leapt. *Good golly*, I thought. *Was it Rachel? Did she see me and want to talk?*

It was Mr. Pratt. He leered at me, dark eyes glowering under heavy lids. His hair was black and greasy and straggled down his ears and collar. I always felt creepy around him, like he's trying to pry a secret out of me.

"Evening, Nathan Wade," he said.

For some reason, Mr. Pratt always used your full name when addressing you. Maybe it had something to do with reading envelopes every day.

"Good evening, Mr. Pratt."

"I hear your cousin David Bushnell is back in town," he said.

"Well, not yet, sir. He's supposed to be on the stagecoach tonight."

"What's he going to be doing with himself now that he's graduated?"

"I really don't know his plans, sir," I said. "I haven't talked to him."

"Indeed," Mr. Pratt said. "I'd have thought he'd join the Continental Army in Boston. Yale's supposed to be full of patriots."

"I've heard that, sir. All I know is he's coming back here. Maybe he'll join the new regiment that's forming in New London."

Mr. Pratt grunted. "That would be the Seventh Connecticut Volunteers."

"Yes sir," I said.

"Your father joined?"

"Yes sir, he did."

"Haven't seen any letters from you lately, Nathan Wade. I'm sure your father would like to hear from you."

"Yes sir, I'm sure he would," I said. Actually I was sure he wouldn't, but I wasn't about to tell that to creepy Mr. Pratt.

He dismissed me with a wave of his hand and I trotted off. I was as eager to see David as I was to get away from Mr. Pratt.

My long legs quickly ate up the five miles to the farm. I hesitated before splashing over the Pochaug. Compared to the Connecticut, the Pochaug is just a creek, and I don't mind it much. It's deep water that scares me.

I ran up the hill to the Bushnells' house and went inside.

David was standing by the fire, his usual tall, skinny self. His raven-black hair just covered his collar. His eyes are gray like the sea is sometimes, and endlessly curious.

"Nate the great," he said, smiling. "It's about time. I was just showing Elias and Mama the design for my science project."

Uncle Elias and Aunt Sarah were bent over the kitchen table, studying a large piece of paper that was covered with a diagram, sketches, and notes.

"I thought it was a secret," I whispered.

"Well, I had to show *somebody*," David said. "I've been working on this thing for two years and haven't told a soul."

I walked over to the table and squeezed in between the two adults like a piglet trying to get a teat from a sow.

The diagram showed a large onion-shaped object with two pipes and a screw curling out the top. Next to them, a fan twirled. Another fan jutted out in front of the object. What appeared to be a large, barrel-shaped trunk was attached to the back. Inside, a man sat on a beam, turning a crank that moved one of the fans.

I didn't know what it was, but I loved it with my whole heart.

Elias's thick eyebrows curled around his eyes. He tugged irritably at his beard. "*This* is it?" he asked. "This is what you couldn't tell us about for a whole year?"

David's eyes glowed excitedly. "This is it." He looked down fondly at the drawing. I could tell he was imagining the thing doing whatever it was supposed to do.

"So what is it?" I asked. "Does it fly? Swim?"

David laughed.

"Yes, Nate, in a manner of speaking it swims," he said. "It's called a submarine. It travels underwater."

I've lived by the Sound all my life and seen all kinds of boats: whaleboats, flatboats, rowboats, and in the last few years, massive British men-o-war. But I'd never seen a boat that could go underwater.

"How can a boat go underwater unless it sinks?" I asked.

"By controlling the sinking," David said, pointing at the bottom of the craft. "The pilot works this valve with his foot and it lets water in and the submarine submerges. This pump pushes the water back out — and up you go."

Aunt Sarah interrupted. "How do you breathe, David?" she asked. "Wouldn't you suffocate in such a small space?"

David tapped the two pipes at the top of the craft. "These let in fresh air while the craft is on the surface," he said. "You surface when the air starts getting stale. Little valves automatically open when you surface and close when you go underwater."

"How's it move?" Elias asked. "You've got no sails and no oars."

"This propeller at the top moves you up and down. This one on the front moves you forward and backward."

We all stared at the object for a minute, puzzling.

Finally Uncle Elias burst out, "I know what it does!" He looked around the table at us, triumphant. "You drag a net behind it to catch the fish! That way you don't have to drag them to the surface by hand."

We all looked at David.

"Nope."

"I know, I know," Aunt Sarah said. "It's a treasure hunter. You can dive down in the Sound looking for sunken gold."

We all looked at David.

"No again."

We studied the submarine for a few more minutes.

"What's this?" I asked finally, pointing to the trunk-shaped thing on the back.

"That's the bomb," David said.

The room got very quiet.

"The *bomb?*" Aunt Sarah asked, aghast.

"Yes. It'll carry one hundred and fifty pounds of gunpowder." David smiled. "I found a way to explode gunpowder underwater."

Embers popped in the fireplace, and we all jumped a little.

"Oh, I see," I said. "You detach the bomb and it blows

up underwater. Then the blown-up fish float to the top, and you scoop 'em up."

I liked this idea a lot. If I brought this water machine home and it helped Papa's business, I'd be a hero.

"It's not for fishing, Nate," David said.

The glow flickered out of David's eyes. I could see his imagination returning from the high seas to the little kitchen.

"Well, what's it for then?" Aunt Sarah asked.

"It's for blowing up British ships," David said solemnly.

Aunt Sarah sucked in her breath. Uncle Elias's hand started pulling at his beard again.

"That's what I couldn't tell you in my letters," David said. "It's for the war. I couldn't trust saying anything in the mail. A spy might read it and I'd be exposed."

"Blow up ships?" Uncle Elias asked. "You mean warships?"

"Of course," David said. "What else would I blow up? The Connecticut fishing fleet? There's a war on, you know."

We all chewed on that for a minute.

Uncle Elias shook his head. "David, one cannon shot hits this contraption of yours, and you'll be fish food at full fathom five."

"But that's the beauty of it, Elias," David said. "The submarine will sneak right up on them underwater. They'll never see it. It's pure stealth."

David pointed to the long screw that extended from the submarine.

"See?" said David, excitement returning to his voice. "The bomb is attached to the screw by this rope. You twist the screw into the bottom of the boat. Then you detach the bomb from the submarine by pulling out this rod, which also sets off a timer. You've got an hour to make your getaway before the bomb blows up."

"And I suppose you'll be the pilot," Uncle Elias said.

David nodded slightly. "I guess."

Uncle Elias sighed and let go of his beard. "David, you can't fight the whole British navy," he said. "It's the best in the world. You're only one man."

"So was David when he took on Goliath," David said. "He took him down with a little rock. I'm thirty-three, Elias, and this is what I want do for the Revolution. Inventing is what I'm good at."

Elias chuckled softly. "David, only you would dream of taking on the biggest navy in the world with a science project."

David looked at us sternly. "You can't tell anyone," he said. "I know most folks around here are for independence, but it just takes one person loyal to the British Crown, one measly Tory spy to find out, and I'd be ruined."

I nodded, trying to look serious. Actually, I felt

ashamed. David was going to take on the greatest navy in the world with something that had never been done before.

Me? I was afraid to fight Butch Hyde. What good was I going to be in the Revolution?

Chapter 2

Uncle Elias yawned. "Time for bed, my turtledove," he sang out to Aunt Sarah.

David picked up a lantern and walked to the door. "C'mon, Nate," he said. "Let's go for a walk."

We walked over one of the fields toward the barn. I breathed in the smell of summer corn. I followed David and the lantern down a row, the cornstalks reaching my knees.

When we got to the barn, David lifted the latch of the

big door and we went inside. Light from the lantern wobbled up and down the walls; a rat skittered through a broken slat. The scent of old straw and manure tingled faintly in my nostrils.

"I haven't been in here in forever," David said. He chuckled. "And I sure haven't missed it. Boy, I hated farming."

"Well, you haven't missed much," I said, sitting on an old milk stool. "Hoeing and weeding, hoeing and weeding, hoeing and weeding."

David sat down on the edge of a wooden feeding trough. Artemus glanced at us with mild interest, then went back to chewing her cud.

"Artemus, old girl, still making milk after all these years," David said, scratching the cow's head. "I hope I'm that productive when I'm your age."

"David, if you keep coming up with ideas like this water machine, maybe when you're old you'll create a flying machine," I said.

David grinned. "That's not a bad idea. If we're still at war with England when I'm old, I'll drop bombs on the British fleet from the flying machine."

I could see David's mind whirring, trying to visualize a flying machine. I decided I'd better pull his brain back into the barn before it was too late.

"So what in the world made you want to build a *sub-*

marine?" I asked, my mouth struggling to form the strange word.

"Well, I needed something to carry the bomb. The submarine was sort of an afterthought. When it looked like we were really going to war, I started experimenting at Yale with setting off gunpowder underwater. The first time I set off two ounces. When that worked, I started making bigger and bigger bombs, and they worked too." David shrugged. "But what good is an underwater bomb if you can't get it out to the ship to set it off?"

"Why not just tow it out with a boat?" I asked.

"Too obvious. The British would blow you out of the water before you got within five hundred yards of them. Even if you did get close enough, you'd still make a racket attaching the bomb and they'd shoot you. I needed something that would be invisible to the watchmen."

"So the submarine just sneaks up on ships, attaches the bomb, and sneaks out?"

"Exactly. Like I told Elias, this is pure stealth."

For a moment I forgot my fear of the water and imagined myself pedaling the submarine out to attack British men-o-war menacing the Connecticut coast. I would return a hero after sinking half the fleet. Of course, Rachel Pratt would be among the hundreds cheering my triumphant return.

"Nate." There was something serious in David's tone

that sank my daydream faster than I'd been sinking men-o-war.

"Nate," he repeated. "I need help building this thing. I'm only one man. This thing is going to be big. When we're finished, it'll weigh about a ton — literally. You saw the diagram. It's got lots of parts and is going to take lots of work."

"Why don't you ask Ezra?" I asked. David's brother seemed an obvious choice to me. He was six years younger than David, and strong from years of farming. Sometimes David was sickly, and it seemed like Ezra was always behind him, shoring him up.

"Oh, Ezra is going to help all right. But he's joining up with the new regiment over in New London and is going to be gone some. I need help beyond Ezra. I'd like you to be the one."

I was flattered — I was being asked to help in the war! Just as quickly a fearful thought struck.

"Would I have to get in the water?" I asked.

David sat back down on the trough. "Not if you don't want to. You know my health isn't the best, so I need all the help I can get. You and Ezra can help haul equipment, find things, troubleshoot. . . ."

We were quiet a minute, thinking. "I wonder if you'd like the sea if you gave it a chance," David said. "You're the son of a fisherman; it just seems natural."

"Hey, you're the son of a farmer, and you aren't exactly farming."

"Quite true. It's just that you don't seem to fit with farming either. You know what I mean?"

"I did give fishing a chance last spring," I said defensively. "I got so scared, I curled up in the bottom of the boat, and they had to pry me out."

David covered his mouth with his hand, suppressing a laugh. "I heard about it, Nate."

"I guess everyone in New England heard," I said bitterly. "The post riders probably took word all the way to Boston."

"You know why you're scared of water, don't you?" David asked.

I looked at him, surprised.

"Didn't anyone ever tell you?" he asked.

"Tell me what?" I asked hesitantly, pretty darn sure I didn't want to know.

"You almost drowned when you were five. We were taking the ferry over the river to Lyme. When no one was looking, you fell in. You probably saw a fish and were trying to grab it. I heard the splash and saw your face disappearing down into the water."

I suddenly shivered, almost feeling the chilly water on my skin. "I don't remember."

"I sure do, like it was yesterday." David shook his head.

"I dove in and pulled you up. You were coughing and choking, but alive. Lord, we were scared. We thought we'd lost you."

"Even Papa?" I asked.

David shot me a puzzled glance. "Of course your father was scared," he said. "In fact, he was *frantic*."

"Really?" I asked. This didn't sound like the gruff Papa I knew, the Papa who always seemed disappointed with me.

"From that day on you've been scared of water. It even took a while to get you to take a bath. I guess we thought you'd grow out of it."

An overwhelming sense of shame settled over me. I hadn't grown out of it. I was fourteen and *still* scared of water. Why couldn't I have been born in Pennsylvania or Georgia or somewhere where there wasn't so much stinking water?

David changed the subject. "I can't stress enough how secret the submarine is," he said. "If the wrong person finds out, they might even try to kill me, Nate. That's how war is. The submarine will be a weapon of war, which makes me an enemy of the British Crown."

"If anyone finds out, we'll tell them it's a machine for fishing, just like Uncle Elias thought it was," I said. "We'll call it the water machine. Every one around here is used to your strange inventions. They'll just say, 'Oh, it's just David Bushnell,' and go on their way."

"Is that what they say? *'Oh, it's just David Bushnell'?*"

"Well, something like that."

"Wonderful. My name is the embodiment of all things odd." David laughed. "Well, after all these years I'm used to it. Besides, it's true. I'm thirty-three years old and I'm building a — what'd you call it? — water machine. The other men are marching off to war and I'm tinkering around on an underwater boat."

David looked across the barn, considering. "Sometimes I think I should join the army and fight like everyone else," he continued. "But I know I'm supposed to do this. Maybe this is how Noah felt when God told him to build the ark."

"It took Noah one hundred years to build the ark," I said. "I don't think we've got that long."

David laughed. "No we don't," he said. "One hundred *days,* maybe."

We sat quietly in the lantern light, our silhouettes huge on the barn wall.

"So is Butch Hyde still making your life miserable?" David asked.

I reddened at the memory of the day's taunting. "Yeah. Just like every summer, he's been calling me a coward."

"Well, are you?" David asked.

"I'm afraid to fight him, so I guess I am."

David thought for a minute. "I feel like a coward sometimes, too. I'm afraid to build this submarine. A lot of things could go wrong. The British could blow it out of the water. Or it might leak and sink. Some of their men-o-war have sixty-four guns. Can you imagine sixty-four guns blazing away at that little craft?"

"That's different," I said. "You're going to fight for our independence. Butch is just a bully."

"Maybe you're going to have to fight your own war of independence, Nate. Freedom from fear. Freedom from being afraid of Butch."

I sat quietly, wondering how in the world I'd do that.

"I'll make you a deal," David said. "You help me build the submarine, I'll help you take on Butch Hyde. But I won't beat him up for you. Heck, he'd probably beat me up, I'm so skinny. But I'll find a way to help you."

I nodded my head slowly. I wasn't too sure I wanted to take on Butch, with or without help.

But it sure felt good to have hope.

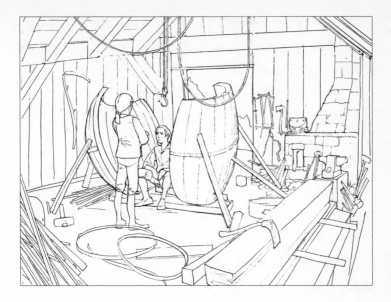

Chapter 3

I heard the river before I saw it, bubbling and gurgling against the shore.

Later that night, David, Ezra, and I were walking down the road from the farm to the river. A half moon hung high in the sky. It was midnight and I was sleepy and irritable.

"Why can't we build it in the barn?" I grumbled.

"Everyone and their dog will find out if we build it in the barn," David said. "You know nothing stays secret in

Saybrook for more than five minutes. We might as well put up a sign that says, 'Calling all Tories, Submarine Being Built Here.'"

"So where *are* we going to build it?"

"We'll be there soon enough," David said.

Ezra and I scurried to keep up with David.

"It's on Poverty Island, out in the middle of the river," Ezra whispered.

"In the middle of the river?" I asked, aghast. "On an island?"

"Yup. It used to be a fisherman's island, but folks don't really go out there anymore."

Ezra was unfazed, but I wasn't. To get to the island, we had to . . . *cross half the river.* And the Connecticut was no Pochaug. I glimpsed the water in the distance — sleek, turbulent, and terrifying.

In a few minutes we arrived at the river's edge. David peered suspiciously at the shadows along the shore while Ezra dragged a small boat out of the reeds.

"Let's go," David said, all business. He and Ezra stepped into the boat. I stood on the shore, trying not to tremble.

"Nate, we don't have all night," David hissed. "You can do this."

"All right," I stammered, shuffling down the bank. I leaned backwards, keeping as much distance between the water and myself as possible. Finally I stepped into the boat. The moment I felt the awkward pulse of water beneath me, I closed my eyes, lurched, and fell. Strong arms caught me. When I opened my eyes, black water rippled a foot from my face. Ezra hauled me up and set me down.

"I'll row going, you row going back," Ezra said to me. Neither he nor David seemed to give a second thought to my blunder.

"Sure," I said, trying to sound casual.

David was scrutinizing the opposite shore.

"Ain't no Tories here, big brother," Ezra said. "This is Connecticut. All the Tories are in New York."

David shook his head. "They're everywhere. I can smell 'em. Lots of people are still loyal to the king, even here."

I could tell I was in the middle of an old argument. Ezra winked at me and pulled hard at the oars. I watched wistfully as the shore quickly receded. Soon we were surrounded by dark, fast-flowing water. I gripped the wood plank seat tightly and tried to act like I wasn't scared.

Powered by Ezra's meaty arms, the boat moved swiftly to the island. In minutes we were stepping out onto a small strip of beach. Poverty Island was about one hundred yards long and fifty yards wide — a speck in the mighty Connecticut. David headed straight for a little grove of trees.

"Come along, gentlemen, we haven't got all night," he said, disappearing into the trees.

Ezra rolled his eyes at me and smiled. "Wait 'til you've gone a couple weeks working days on the farm for Elias and nights for Master Bushnell," he said. "The other day I fell asleep hoeing and woke up with my face in the dirt."

As I slipped into the trees, I understood why David had selected Poverty Island. The trees perfectly concealed the island's interior. It would take a determined spy to find the submarine's hiding place. I followed Ezra into a little clearing where an old shed stood. Yellow lantern light leaked through cracks in the walls.

"If anyone ever sees us, the story is that David has taken up fishing and the shed is for the reel that he winds his net on," Ezra said.

David was sitting on his haunches between two huge pieces of wood. Each was about seven feet long, six feet wide, and shaped like a tortoise shell. I recognized them instantly from David's drawing — the outer shell of the submarine.

"It's made of oak timbers, six inches thick," David said, standing up. "Tonight we'll finish fastening the timbers together. I found an ironmonger in Lyme to make some iron bands. In a couple days we'll seal the joints with cork and plaster the whole thing with tar. It's got to be tight as a drum, no leaks."

"That's good to hear since I'll be manning this thing," Ezra said.

When I gave David a confused look, he explained. "I've decided I can't take on the redcoats all by myself." He slapped Ezra on the shoulder. "I'm going to let my little brother pilot my machine."

"Your health . . . ," I began.

"And of course, I've got to finish rigging the explosive device," David said, abruptly changing the subject. "I'm going to New Haven in a few weeks to meet with a man who is going to make the clock that sets the bomb off."

"How'd you get it done so fast?" I asked. "You just got back from Yale yesterday."

"I actually started working on it last summer. Ezra and I got a lot done. When the fighting started at Lexington, I was tempted to drop out of school and finish the submarine. But I've wanted my degree for so long. . . ."

David shrugged, a guilty look in his eyes. "A lot of the boys went to Boston to join the Army. It got real hard when General Washington stopped by New Haven and the Yale regiment drilled for him. I wanted to follow him all the way to Boston to fight the blasted British. But I stayed put and got my degree. Now I want to put that to good use."

"You know, we really ought to name this thing, David," Ezra said. "'Submarine' doesn't have much of a ring to it."

David seemed puzzled. "A name? That never occurred to me. But I guess they do name ships."

He looked at me. "Doesn't your father's boat have a name?"

"The *Claire Diana*," I said, quiet-like.

"Nah, not manly enough," David said. "How about the *Israel Putnam*? Or the –" He must have seen something in my eyes because he shut up suddenly. "I'm sorry, Nathan. I forgot that Claire was your mother's name."

"It's all right," I said. "It's been a long time."

I shook off the sadness and looked at the two halves of the submarine lying on the dirt floor. "It looks just like a turtle," I said brightly.

David chortled. "You're right, Nate. It *does* look like a turtle!"

He rubbed his chin thoughtfully. "But it still needs something else. Something revolutionary. . . . I know! Let's call it the *American Turtle*. We're Americans fighting for America, and this is *our* submarine."

Ezra didn't seem impressed. "Well, gents, that's a lovely, if unromantic name, but personally I'd like to get more done tonight than naming this little contraption."

Strong-as-an-ox Ezra heaved one of the halves, while David and I hoisted up the other. While I held our half steady, David went outside and retrieved several large logs. He wedged one against each side of the submarine, placing the end of each log in small holes dug into the floor.

"All right, let her go," David said.

We stepped back and I felt a surge of pride. The submarine, the *American Turtle,* stood in one whole piece. She was round like an onion, not so turtle-ish now, about a foot taller than me. For the next several hours we worked quietly, sweating in the stuffy little shed. We fitted iron bands around the submarine, sealing the two halves tightly together.

"I've really missed working on this thing," David said. "It's taken over my mind. I've gone over every inch of it, figured out how to make every valve and pipe work, how to make the bomb work. . . ."

David paused, and when he spoke again the menace in his tone startled me.

"It's *got* to work," he said. "We've *got* to strike those British for what they're doing. They've invaded us, they're taxing us to high heaven. We've got to fight back and drive them out of America."

I'd heard talk like David's for a long time. Everyone in New London read newspapers and talked about British oppression and "taxation without representation." Papa went down to the Green Dragon Tavern every night and grumbled with the other men about British taxes on tea. Post riders galloped down from Boston with the latest news on the war.

The war made everyone angry and suspicious all the time. You wondered who was a patriot and who was a

Tory. Some people, like David, were spoiling for a fight. Some secretly sided with the British. And some flat didn't care. They just wanted to be left alone. It was strange not knowing if you could trust folks you'd known your whole life.

All these different opinions confused me. I didn't like that the British taxed everything, and they were wrong to kill our men at Lexington and Concord and Bunker Hill. But other folks talked about how they were our fellow countrymen, how we were all English.

David interrupted my thoughts. "The only thing that can stop us is Tories," he said. "One slip of the tongue could sink us — literally. You can't tell anyone. . . . One Tory spy could ruin everything. We're talking life and death. You can't even tell your father or your friends. No one. Do you hear me? No one."

I nodded. The "life and death" thing kind of scared me. Would they really kill you just for building a boat?

It was like David was reading my mind. He pointed to the submarine in the flickering lantern light.

"We're in a war, and this is a weapon of that war," he said. "By creating the *Turtle*, we've become combatants. We are now the enemy of the British empire."

Ezra and I let that sink in. Finally Ezra spoke.

"Well, what do you say that we get on with building

this weapon of war? I'd like to get a whole three hours of sleep tonight."

David grunted and stood up. "Nathan, go out and take a look around and see if the coast is clear. Ezra and I will finish up."

I was hot and tired and glad for a chance to go outside. I stepped through the trees to the little beach. The river flowed by, dark and strong and threatening. The moon dimly lit the shoreline for several miles. Jutting out in the distance was Sill's Point. The Saybrook Ferry — where I'd almost drowned nine years ago — was just beyond.

Suddenly I spotted a shadowy form moving on the far shore where our boat had been hidden. Was it a deer or a man? *Oh God, let it be a deer.* The shadow stopped and seemed to stare straight across the water at me.

Dang, it can't be a deer. Deer don't stand on two legs. In fact, the thick form looked eerily like Mr. Pratt. Heart racing, I ducked behind a bush and peeked through the branches. The riverbank was empty, just reeds and trees swaying in the soft wind.

I crawled back to the shed. David and Ezra, who were tightening down the iron band, looked up.

"Nate, why are you crawling?" David asked.

"I saw someone on the shore," I whispered.

David was instantly agitated. "I knew it!" he exclaimed. "Someone found us out!"

Ezra yawned. "It was probably a deer," he said. "Wasn't it, Nate? Just a thirsty deer getting a drink?"

"Nope, it stared across the water straight at me," I said. "It stood on two legs."

David snuffed out the lantern and the shed went dark. I turned and smacked my face straight into the stout side of the *Turtle*.

"Yow!" I yelled.

"Quiet!" David hissed. "We've got to sneak farther downriver so the spy can't see us."

"Oh great," Ezra groaned. "That adds another mile to our walk home. We'll be just in time for breakfast. C'mon David, it's probably just someone out for a walk wondering what fools are out on the island at two in the morning."

To mask our escape, we dragged the boat to the other side of the island. We made a glorious racket crushing bushes and snapping dead tree branches, but finally got the boat in the water and floated off. About a mile downstream, Ezra steered us toward the western shore. We saw and heard nothing.

"Are you sure you saw something, Nate?" David asked. "The shoreline has a lot of shadows, and it's only a half moon."

"Maybe my eyes were playing tricks on me, but it sure looked like a man." I didn't add that I thought it was Mr. Pratt.

"Coast is clear, Cap'n," Ezra said to David.

We climbed out of the boat, and this time when it lurched I kept my balance. At David's direction, Ezra waded into a deep thicket of reeds and tied the boat to a submerged tree.

"Let our Tory spy find *that*," David said.

I was bone tired. As we trudged the long miles home, I didn't think about the submarine or the Revolution or Butch Hyde or being afraid of water. All I could think of was sliding into my warm bed in the cozy loft.

But then I thought of Rachel Pratt and my sagging eyelids popped wide open. If that *was* her father watching us, then he was probably a Tory. And if he was a Tory, what did that make her? And if I was in love with Rachel, what did that make me?

Criminey, I thought, *this war just keeps getting more and more complicated.*

It was July, and the submarine was looking like, well, whatever a submarine was supposed to look like. Night after night we sweated in the little shed. Then we traipsed home, slept a few hours, got up, and worked the farm. Some nights I was so sleepy Ezra had to poke me awake with whatever tool he was holding.

As the *Turtle* grew, so did my excitement. We were developing a mighty weapon of war and I wanted to brag about it to Josh in the worst way. Even more, I wanted to rub Butch Hyde's face in it. "See," I imagined myself saying, "you're not the only one who knows how to fight!"

But I don't think a night went by that David didn't remind us how important it was to keep the *Turtle* a secret. "See any Tories?" he'd ask, looking up and down the riverbanks.

In my fatigue I hardly even cared. But maybe that's because it was David's hide on the line and not mine. Tories wouldn't mess with a fourteen-year-old, would they? Weeks passed, and we didn't see Mr. Pratt, or a Tory, or even a wandering deer.

While David worked on the submarine's instruments, Ezra and I waterproofed the exterior. First we packed the seams between the two tortoise-shaped halves tight with cork. Then we slathered the surface of the submarine with layers of gooey tar.

"Lay it on thick, Nate," Ezra said. "If I'm going underwater in this thing, it'd better be leak proof." He winked at me. "I've always said there's nothing worse than a leaky submarine."

If Ezra was scared about going underwater, he didn't show it. If it had been me going down, I'd have been petrified. Just thinking about being in water made me shiver, even in the hot shed. I thought about poor Ezra bumping around in the deep currents, crammed into the little craft. *What if it did leak?* I slapped on more tar, scouring the surface for spots we might have missed. Ezra would surely drown if the *Turtle* leaked, even a tiny bit. And David wouldn't be able to reach down and yank him up like he did with me nine years ago.

Suddenly David's head popped up out of the top of the machine.

"Gentlemen, I present the depth gauge!" David loved showing off his inventions, and since the *Turtle* was a secret, Ezra and I were his only audience.

David held up a glass tube. It was about eighteen inches long and an inch wide; the upper end was sealed shut. Little lines were painted on the side of the tube, and a piece of cork was wedged inside.

"This will be attached to the wall in front of the pilot's seat," David said. "The open end will be attached to a pipe that runs outside the submarine. When the *Turtle* descends, water will enter through the pipe into the gauge. The air pressure in the tube will keep the water from completely filling it. I've calculated that for every six feet the *Turtle* descends, the cork will rise one inch."

"What good is a depth gauge when you can't read it?" Ezra asked, grinning. "Maybe when I hit the bottom of the Sound I'll know how deep I am, huh David?"

David grunted and waved Ezra off. "I'll figure something out," he said.

"What's the problem?" I asked.

"I can't see in the dark, that's the problem," Ezra said. "We're going to launch the *Turtle* at night, and it's going to be pitch black underwater. Without light I won't be able to see where I'm going or read the compass or use this fancy depth thing."

"How about a candle?" I asked. "That would give plenty of light."

"It would eat up too much air," David said in a muffled voice. He had dropped down into the *Turtle* again. "By my estimate, the *Turtle* only has about thirty minutes of air underwater." He paused. "You'll have to paddle quick, Ezra."

Ezra rolled his eyes. "This is starting to sound like a lot of fun. I get to paddle in the dark, hope I don't suffocate, and avoid British cannon. You're going to have to make this up to me, big brother."

As we worked, I thought about the problems of darkness and air. If we didn't find answers, the *Turtle* might be sunk before it was launched. Then the name of the most famous man in the Colonies popped into my head: Dr. Benjamin Franklin. He had invented a lot of things. He'd even discovered electricity! How hard could it be to illuminate a little seven-by-six-foot underwater boat? For Dr. Franklin, it would be a cinch!

"David, what if you wrote to Benjamin Franklin and asked him how to light the *Turtle*?" I asked. "He discovered electricity with a kite. Surely he could come up with something for the submarine."

David's head popped up. "Benjamin Franklin? You've *got* to be joking. What would he want to do with me?"

"Seems like he's interested in everything, especially inventions," I said, placing my hands affectionately on the *Turtle*. "I bet there's nothing like this in the whole world. I think he'd be interested."

"I doubt it," David said, shaking his head. "Dr. Franklin is in Philadelphia with the Continental Congress. He doesn't have time for something small like this."

"I don't know," Ezra said. "I've read that he relaxes by working out complicated math problems. He could probably knock out our little light problem during lunch."

"Gentlemen, drop it," David said sharply, lowering himself back into the submarine. "I will find a solution to the lighting problem in due time. Now can we get back to work?"

As we walked home that night, I considered writing to Benjamin Franklin myself. What would a letter from a fourteen-year-old boy mean to the most famous man in America? Probably nothing. He likely got lots of letters from important people. . . . But how many letters did he get about submarines?

The more I thought about it, the more the idea of writing Dr. Franklin made sense. But deep down a doubt lingered. I had promised David I wouldn't tell anyone about the *Turtle*. But couldn't Dr. Franklin be an exception? After all, he was one of the leaders of the Revolution, and if anyone was a patriot, he was.

*   *   *

The next day I snuck out to the barn with a pen and ink and paper.

Dear Dr. Franklin,

My cousin David Bushnell in Saybrook, Connecticut, is an inventor like you. He has invented a water machine to fight the British. It travels underwater and can attach gunpowder bombs to ships. The bombs actually explode underwater. He knows they work because he tried them out at Yale. We have a problem I thought you could help us with. It's dark underwater and we need light so we can see the depth gauge and compass. A candle won't work because it would burn up all the air. Do you have any ideas?

Your obedient servant,
Nathan Wade
Saybrook, Connecticut

The next day I rode into Saybrook on the wagon with David and Uncle Elias.

"Letter for your father?" Uncle Elias asked, nodding toward the envelope in my hand.

"Uh, yes," I lied. "Just telling him how the crops are doing."

"So how *are* they doing?" Uncle Elias asked mischievously.

"Good enough, I guess. The corn is up to my knees."

Once we were in town, Uncle Elias and David went into Bower's General Store to get some supplies, and I went down the street to the Rising Sun Tavern. I couldn't believe that I, lowly Nathan Wade, was mailing a letter to the great patriot Benjamin Franklin.

As I neared the tavern, though, my doubts began gnawing at me. What if Mr. Pratt intercepted the letter? I didn't trust him as far as I could spit. Maybe his assistant Mr. Willard would be there instead. Mild as a mug of milk, Mr. Willard would forget whom the letter was addressed to five minutes after reading it. *Well, here goes,* I thought, and stepped into the gloom of the tavern.

"Good day, Nathan."

Whew! It was Mr. Willard. "Good day, Mr. Willard."

"Need to mail that?" he asked, nodding at the letter in my hand.

"Yes sir."

He took the letter from my hand and put it in a bag without even looking at it.

"Sir, when do you think the letter will mail?" I asked.

"Well, there is a post rider down the street. He'll be down here to get our mail unless he's in a hurry with big news."

"A post rider?" I exclaimed. I ran out to the street, leaving the letter and Mr. Willard behind. Uncle Elias and David were hurrying toward a crowd gathered at the wharf. I ran to catch up with them.

Riders rode fast horses up and down the Post Road, bringing news to the towns along the way. The road stretched from Boston down to New London, then west along the coast through Saybrook to New Haven and then on to New York City.

I saw Josh's short, tubby body running to meet us. "Independence!" he yelled. "The Continental Congress signed a Declaration of Independence on July Fourth! The Colonies are free!"

David cracked a big grin and leaned in close to my ear. "It's almost time for the *Turtle* to fulfill its mission," he whispered.

As the crowd cheered, the post rider galloped off to take the wonderful news to New Haven. When the hard-charging horse neared the Rising Sun, Mr. Pratt leapt out into the street. He was waving an envelope. The startled rider yanked back hard on the reins. He shouted at Mr.

Pratt, who kept waving the envelope. I was too far away to hear what was said, but the rider finally snatched the envelope from Mr. Pratt's hand and thundered down the road.

My stomach started swirling. Dang, Mr. Pratt was there after all! What letter was so important for him to almost tackle the post rider? I couldn't help but worry that it was my letter to Dr. Franklin.

While Uncle Elias and David hustled home in the wagon to tell Ezra and Aunt Sarah, I walked Josh home.

"See you, Nate," he said, walking to his front door. "Get some sleep, all right? You look terrible. What, is David keeping you up all night inventing stuff?"

"Yeah, something like that," I mumbled.

As soon as Josh closed the door, my fears about the letter came barreling back. What if Mr. Pratt had read it? Why had I written the letter in the first place? David would have figured out the lighting problem by himself.

I stood still, the pieces falling together in my mind. It *had* been Mr. Pratt I'd seen that night on the river. It was dark, sure, but I'd recognize that ugly old slouch shape anywhere. Why hadn't I believed myself? So he was a Tory. He'd almost certainly read my letter to Dr. Franklin. Then he'd written a note to the British telling them about the *Turtle*. Finally, he forced the post rider to take the letter.

Sheesh, this was bad. We were exposed! They would hang David and Ezra, they would sabotage the *Turtle*, and they would . . . tar and feather me? How long before the letter got to the British? A few days . . . a few weeks?

Anger boiled up inside me. That old goat Pratt! I had to warn David. As I started to run, a leg shot out from the side of the Pratts' house. I sprawled headfirst, my jaw banging against the hard-packed dirt street. Pain racked my head, and I tasted blood.

"What's your hurry, yellowbelly?" Butch Hyde's boot was on the back of my head, grinding my face into the dirt. "You running home to your chicken cousin who ain't got the guts to fight redcoats?"

Suddenly from above I heard a voice — a female voice. "Butch, you leave him alone!"

Startled, Butch lifted his boot off my head. I spat bloody saliva and looked up. A window on the second floor framed long red hair and a pretty, angry face. *Great,* I thought. *Rachel was finally looking down from her window at me — and I was getting whipped.*

"Butch, you coward!" she yelled.

"Oh shut up, Pratt," Butch snapped. "Wade is bigger than me and you know it. He's too scared to fight."

"Then why do you pick on him? What are you scared of?"

"You're one to talk. How about you and your whole turn-coat family? Your father's a Tory, and everyone knows it."

Rachel's eyes flamed with fury and, I wondered, tears?

"He is not, you ugly son of an ironmonger!" she yelled, now definitely crying.

Then I did something I couldn't believe. I flipped onto my back and whipped my legs as hard as I could at Butch's legs. He dropped like a corn stalk cut by a sharp scythe. Butch landed heavily next to me, his face barely six inches from mine. For a second we just sort of looked at each other in disbelief — him because I'd leveled him, me because, well, I'd actually leveled him.

Out of the corner of my eye I saw his fist heading for my head. In an instant I was on my feet running for the woods behind the village.

"You're just like Pratt, a yellowbelly Tory!" Butch yelled.

I stopped dead in my tracks and slowly turned around. *Tory?* I thought angrily. *Tory?* I work every night until three o'clock building a weapon of war for the Continental Army, and he calls me a Tory? I wanted to scream, "I'm building a submarine, you" — what had Rachel said? — "ugly son of an ironmonger idiot!"

But just as the retort rose in my throat, I remembered David's words: "It just takes one Tory spy to find out and we'll be ruined." Butch was no Tory, but I knew he'd flap his lip and tell everyone in town about the *Turtle*.

I turned and dashed into the woods. When I was sure Butch wasn't pursuing, I slowed to a walk. My tongue was cut, and drying blood crusted on my chin. Dusk was gathering. I sat in a little clearing and listened to the growing racket of the cicadas.

Little pricks of light — fireflies — began flickering around the clearing. *Too bad we couldn't bottle some of them to light the submarine,* I thought. Once I'd mashed up a bunch of them and tried to light the barn, but the faint yellow glow had faded in a few seconds.

I thought about this for a minute and then an idea hit me: *Foxfire!* Why hadn't we thought of it before? Foxfire could light the submarine!

I got up and pushed into the woods. I soon saw what I was looking for: a faint glow on the ground. Hacking through undergrowth, I reached a rotting log. Soft flecks of light speckled the crumbling wood. With my knife I scraped off some of the luminous, mossy stuff.

We could attach pieces of foxfire on the depth gauge and compass. I was sure it would work in the submarine, if the Tories hadn't sunk it yet. The memory of my foolish letter to Benjamin Franklin flooded back. *If only I'd waited before sending the letter,* I thought. The answer had been right in front me!

David was going to kill me — if the Tories didn't kill him first.

Chapter 5

When I got home everyone was sitting by the fire.

"Catching fireflies, Nathan?" Uncle Elias asked.

"Uh, sort of." I held out my hand full of moss. "It's foxfire, for the depth gauge and compass."

David beamed at me. "Nate, that's great, just great!" he exclaimed. "And *you* wanted to write Benjamin Franklin for a solution."

"Yeah," I mumbled, "How silly of me. What was I thinking?"

"Well, the foxfire is the missing piece to our puzzle," David said. "We're almost ready to test the *Turtle*."

"Elijah Fenton just got back from New York," Ezra said. "He says the harbor is packed with British ships, at least a couple of hundred. Someone told him it's the greatest expedition the British ever launched. General Washington sure has his hands full."

David's eyes lit up. "It'll be like shooting fish in a barrel!"

"More like blowing up fish in a barrel, don't you think?" Uncle Elias asked, furry eyebrows arched.

"That would be more accurate," David said. "Of course, there's no way we can attack two or three hundred ships. But if we hit one or two, it might put a scare in the rest of 'em, and maybe they'd leave. It'd take the pressure off the Continentals."

Uncle Elias nodded and looked at the fire thoughtfully. "I think you should go after Admiral Richard Howe," he said. "Sink the flagship and kill the top man. That would send a message to King George, by God."

"Can you imagine how scared the lobsterbacks will be when their ships start blowing up in the middle of the night?" Ezra asked. "For no apparent reason?"

Uncle Elias nodded. "That's the beauty of the *Turtle*," he said. "It's something no one has ever seen in a war before. They'll have no idea what hit them."

"That's why we have to keep everything so secret," David said. "If they find out how lethal the *Turtle* is they'll stop at nothing to destroy it."

Minutes later we were stretched out on our straw mattresses in the loft. I heard the deep breathing of Ezra; he always fell asleep in about four seconds. I usually fell fast asleep too, but my guilt about writing to Benjamin Franklin hung heavily over me. I turned this way and that, burrowing into the straw like a pig. But nothing worked.

"Nathan, what's the matter?" David whispered.

I was surprised that David was still awake. He was the last person I wanted to talk to. "Well, uh, Butch beat me up today . . . in front of Rachel." It wasn't a total lie, I reasoned. I'd been so worried about the letter that I hadn't had time to worry about my next beating from Butch.

I told David what had happened with Butch.

"Doesn't sound so bad to me," he said. "Heck, you knocked him on his back. You've never done that before."

I hadn't thought of it that way. "Yeah, but it was in front of Rachel . . . and I was the one who ran away."

"But you stuck up for her, remember? You went after him when he said that stuff about her father. I bet she noticed that."

I hadn't thought of that either.

"Go to sleep, Nate. You're going to need your rest.

We've got to test the *Turtle* and get it down to New York. The enemy is waiting."

I closed my eyes. Well, that was one worry fixed, even if I hadn't worried about it yet. David was right. I *had* stuck up for Rachel. And if I'd done it once, maybe I could do it again. I stretched. In the faint firelight I saw my toes poking out from the end of the blanket. They seemed so far away. I squinted: they were far away. *Hey,* I thought, *I* am *big, bigger than Butch.* So why did I always feel so small?

David must have heard me sighing. "What's the matter now?"

"Nothing," I said.

"I can't sleep either."

"Why?"

"I'm thinking through the tests. I want to make sure everything works."

I thought of the letter again for the umpteenth time that day. *Dang!* It was probably hoofing its way right now to a British officer in New York.

In a split second I decided to blurt out the truth. "David, I did write Benjamin Franklin about the *Turtle.*"

For a few moments all I heard was Ezra snoring. "Benjamin Franklin? Really? *The* Benjamin Franklin?" David sounded pleased, not angry.

"I thought you might need help lighting the depth gauge and compass."

David laughed. "I can't believe you wrote Benjamin Franklin about my little invention."

"I figured if anyone could help, he could."

David chuckled again, amused. "Yeah, I guess the greatest inventor in the world could figure out how to light an underwater boat."

"I'm sorry, David. I know it was supposed to be a secret."

"Well, Nate, no harm done. Dr. Franklin is hardly a Tory."

David was in a good mood; I decided to drop my bomb. "No, but I think Mr. Pratt is."

"Pratt? What's he got to do with this?"

"I think he may have read the letter."

"You think he read the letter." David repeated slowly.

"You remember the post rider?"

David slumped back on the mattress. "Yes, I remember the rider. . . . So you think he sent a warning to the British about the *Turtle?*"

"Wouldn't you if you were a Tory?"

"Yeah. . . . That weasel."

David laid back down quietly, thinking for a few minutes. Suddenly he sat up and nudged Ezra. "Wake up, little brother. We've got work to do."

Chapter 6

"Intake valve!" Ezra called out.

I was sitting inside the submarine in the middle of Oyster Cove. The *Turtle*, tethered to the rowboat, bobbed gently in the shallow water. Two weeks had passed since the post rider had hoofed off toward New York. So far, no redcoats or Tories had shown up.

It was a good thing, too. The *Turtle* wasn't quite ready. As soon as Ezra took it out in the shallow waters of the cove, problems began popping up. First, the fresh air ventilator failed to push out the stale air in the submarine. Then the pumps that forced water out of the ballast tank so the submarine could ascend malfunctioned. Agitated, David went to work. The problems were finally solved, but precious time had slipped by.

The other issue was that we were working in broad daylight. David decided it was better to risk someone seeing us than to slow down the repairs by working only at night. "It's probably not a secret anymore if Pratt knows," David growled from the rowboat. "I'm surprised half the town isn't out here."

I worked the intake valve lever with my foot and heard water gurgling into the ballast tank. The craft began descending. "Whoa!" yelled Ezra. "We don't want this thing going under just yet."

"Check!" I hollered.

"Ballast pumps!" Ezra called. I worked the ballast pump with my hand and forced the water back out. The *Turtle* began to rise.

"Check."

"Vertical oars!" Ezra called.

I twirled the hand crank to the topside oars. Looking out the open hatch, I saw the oars spinning around. "Check."

"Horizontal oars," Ezra said. I twirled the other hand crank. "Check," Ezra called, since I couldn't see them from inside the submarine.

"Depth gauge and compass."

The two instruments were right in front of my face. David had fastened little strips of foxfire onto them.

"Check."

As we went through the rest of the checklist, I mentally rehearsed how to operate the submarine. *Push the intake valve down to submerge. Operate the upper hand crank to move the vessel deeper. Use lower hand crank to move forward. Push out the water from the ballast tank with the pump.* It was a lot to remember — I was glad I wasn't Ezra.

"Gentlemen," David called out, "we've got company."

I popped my head out of the submarine. Ezra was shading his eyes against the sun, squinting at the shore one hundred feet away. "It's Elias and Mama and an old man." He looked at David and laughed. "Guess we're safe, big brother. They don't look too much like Tories."

"Go see what they want," David muttered irritably.

"Oh, and you're going to cram into the *Turtle* with Nate while I'm gone?"

"All right. We'll both go. You row."

David looked at me. "You going to be all right, Nate? We'll be back in a few minutes."

"Sure," I said, not sure at all. As the rowboat pulled away, I felt the old, familiar fear rise. I was surrounded by water and no one was around to help. I sat down and pulled my feet up, taking great care not to accidentally bump the intake valve.

From one of the windows I watched my cousins reach the shore. They spoke with Uncle Elias and shook hands with the elderly visitor. The next thing I knew, David, Ezra, and the old man were in the boat rowing toward the *Turtle*.

I popped out of the hatch and grabbed the rope Ezra tossed to me. David was talking eagerly to the man, who seemed just as excited as David.

"Extraordinary!" exclaimed the old man. "This is simply extraordinary, Mr. Bushnell. I would be honored to watch you test it."

"The honor is all mine, Dr. Franklin," David said. "Your timing is perfect. We just finished the final repairs. I was going to take it into deeper waters today and see how it does."

Dr. Franklin! Oh my gosh! He must have gotten the letter after all. *But how?*

"Dr. Franklin, this is Nathan Wade," David said. "Nathan, this is Dr. Benjamin Franklin."

Dr. Franklin was stout, bald on top, with long gray hair on the sides — just like the drawings of him in the *New London Gazette*.

"You would be the letter writer," he said, extending his hand up toward me. "I'm so glad you wrote. The Continental Congress is sending me to New York to inspect the

56

army. Saybrook is on the way, and I couldn't resist stopping by to see . . . the water machine."

"It's a great honor to have you here," David said. "I've been an admirer of yours for years."

"Mr. Bushnell, the honor is all mine. It's a pleasure to meet a man of like mind." David smiled shyly, and mumbled something that sounded like "thank you."

"Nate, let's say you and David exchange places," Ezra said. "It's time for our first test run." I climbed out and David climbed in. A few moments later the *Turtle* began sinking into the inky water. In a minute only the conning tower was above water. David peered out one of the port windows, smiling. He was saying something to me. I read his lips: *Don't be afraid, Nate. Don't be afraid.*

Then with a gurgle the *Turtle* was gone.

Dr. Franklin, Ezra, and I sat quietly in the rowboat, watching the dark water. "Pretty amazing, isn't it?" Ezra said. "A few months ago all we had were two pieces of wood. Now there's a submarine down there, getting ready to wreak havoc on the British."

"And just in time," Dr. Franklin said. "The British are gathering in force in New York Harbor. General Washington needs your help."

We sat and waited. And waited. And waited some more. I was certain the thirty-minute air supply in the *Turtle* was about gone. Still David did not appear.

Ezra stirred anxiously. "C'mon, David," he muttered. "You don't have to check every part the first time."

Finally, the water rippled fifty feet away. The conning tower of the *Turtle* broke the surface. We rowed over, and Ezra opened the hatch. David heaved himself up on his elbows, gulping air. "Gentlemen, . . . it worked . . . perfectly," he gasped.

"Are you all right?" Ezra asked.

David nodded, but his face was deathly white. "The air got a bit stale. I wanted to check everything, and I must have lost track of time."

We rowed toward shore, the *Turtle* in tow. "It's a lot more work than I anticipated," David said. "To work the oars and the rudder simultaneously, know where you are, work the ballast pumps — it's a handful."

He sighed and looked at Ezra. "It's one thing to be in a calm little cove, but I hear New York harbor has lots of currents. I know I'd never make it. I'd probably be pulled out to the Sound and you'd never find me. As much as I want to pilot the *Turtle* and take the risk, I'm glad it's going to be you."

Ezra nodded. "I know. That's what I'm here for. You're the brains, I'm the brawn."

We rowed along in silence. Dr. Franklin was staring intently at the submarine, his wispy hair wafting in the breeze. The sun was setting; the water glittered with orange flame.

"So what was it like down there?" I asked.

"Pitch dark," David said. "Except for the foxfire on the depth gauge and compass, I couldn't see anything. I did it all by feel. It took me a while, but the more I worked with things, the easier it got."

"Foxfire," Dr. Franklin said thoughtfully. "Yes, foxfire would work nicely. In the summer months, anyway. Cold weather kills it. Good thinking, Mr. Bushnell."

David smiled. "Actually, it was Nathan's idea."

"Really?" Dr. Franklin said. "Splendid, young man. I guess inventing runs in the family." I swelled up like a frog with pride.

"My own thinking was along the line of fireflies," Dr. Franklin said. "If you caught thousands of them and hung them in bottles in the submarine, you could get quite a glow going — for a little while. The problem would be keeping them alive long enough. They die quickly when bottled up. And you can't exactly catch a fresh supply when you're underwater, now can you?"

He chuckled. "And catching that many fireflies would take a lot of men. Maybe you could get the Continental Army to help. But I don't think General Washington would stand for having half his army traipsing about after insects."

Dr. Franklin paused. "I also wondered if you could somehow capture the little sparks of light you see in the water," he said. "You boys live by the sea. You know what I'm talking about."

Indeed I did, even with as little time as I'd spent on the water. Sometimes at night I'd seen luminous patches of light in the surf.

"I believe the light is caused by a mass of extremely tiny sea creatures. I call them 'animalcules,'" Dr. Franklin said.

"Animalcules?" Ezra asked.

"You can't see them with the human eye," Dr. Franklin explained. "At least not until millions of them mass together."

"So you're not even sure animalcules exist?" David asked.

"No, it's just a theory I have, but a theory is the first step toward discovery, as you well know, Mr. Bushnell." Dr. Franklin nodded toward the *Turtle*.

We all looked at the craft, bobbing beside us in the water.

"Lighting the water machine with animalcules presents the same practical problems as the fireflies, however," Dr. Franklin said. "How do you bottle them up and keep them alive long enough?"

He looked at me and smiled. "So, it sounds like foxfire will do very nicely. I was going to respond to your letter, Mr. Wade, but since I was coming this way, I thought I'd just have a chat with you myself."

I looked at David and Ezra. "I wonder why Mr. Pratt sent my letter? I figured he'd just tear it up and send his note about the *Turtle* to the British. Maybe he didn't read it after all."

"Actually, this Mr. Pratt must have seen your letter," Dr. Franklin said. "On the back of the envelope was a note to a Colonel Nelson of the British army. It described your submarine and said it was a threat to the British navy."

Ezra guffawed. "I know what happened! Pratt was probably in such a hurry he accidentally used the envelope addressed to Dr. Franklin instead of a new one so the British never got Pratt's warning."

David looked at me intently. "Nate, I've got a mission for you. If the British never got the message, Pratt must be wondering why they haven't done something. I've got a feeling he's going to take matters into his own hands. I need you to go to his house tonight and see what you can find out."

"Why don't we all go together?" I asked, shivering at the thought of creepy Mr. Pratt.

"Ezra and I've got to get the *Turtle* on a sloop to go down to New York. I found someone to loan us theirs: the boat, the crew, everything. But we've got to move fast. I'd hate to get this close and have that fool Tory destroy years' worth of my work!"

"Well, all right," I said.

"Good! I knew you'd do it. Take the rowboat after we drop off Dr. Franklin. Meet us at midnight on the island. We'll have the *Turtle* ready to go."

Chapter 9

As I rowed downstream toward Saybrook, I thought about my mission. How would I find out what Mr. Pratt was doing? What if he caught me?

As I neared shore, I realized I'd rowed across the river by myself for the first time. What's more, I was rowing strong and hard. I couldn't believe it.

When I was about thirty feet from shore, I heard rustling in the reeds. I saw a dark figure dart away from the bank and disappear toward town. Heart pounding, I rowed into the cover of the reeds. *Why me?* I thought. I would do anything — *anything!* — if I didn't have to chase this man. But that's how I always felt when I was afraid of something.

I tied the boat to a submerged log and sloshed to shore. Whoever it was had a head start. I ran after him, keeping a safe distance behind as he entered Saybrook. He headed straight to Mr. Pratt's house. I slipped into Josh's yard and crept to the Pratts', two houses down. A light shone from an open window, and I heard men's voices.

I walked toward the window, so scared that my legs didn't want to work. They felt like rubber, and my feet dragged like they were stuck in buckets of molasses. Ten feet from the house, my legs completely locked up. I felt like I was frozen in stone. *What did Tories do to you if you got caught?* I'd heard a lot of stories about patriots tarring and feathering Tories. Did Tories do the same to patriots?

"Nathan," a voice whispered from above. In the moonlight I saw a dark shape in the second-story window. "Hide before they see you! They know about the water machine."

"Rachel?" I stammered. How did she know about the *Turtle?*

From the open downstairs window I heard chairs sliding. "Dadgummit!" Mr. Pratt snapped. "Who is that?" His dark, round-shouldered shape filled the doorway.

"Behind the tree, Nathan, *now!*" Rachel hissed. I flung myself behind a huge old oak just in time.

"Pratt, do you see anything?" a voice called from the window. "You think that boy helping Bushnell followed me?"

"Could be," Mr. Pratt said. He was only a few feet away from the tree. "If it is, I'll skin his little hide and tar and feather what's left."

I looked around wildly for a place to escape. No branch hung low enough to climb, and the street was too far away.

"Father, it was me," Rachel called out. "Up here."

"Girl, what in God's name are you doing up?" Mr. Pratt asked.

"I thought I heard the wolf again."

"What wolf?"

"I heard a wolf growling out here a few nights ago. I think he was looking for something to eat."

"It was probably just Josh Laribee's dadgum dog looking for food. I swear you've got no sense, girl. Get back to bed, and don't let me hear any more of this nonsense."

Mr. Pratt went back into the house. I stayed pinned against the tree for a few more minutes, then tiptoed toward the street.

"Hey Wolf!" I looked up and saw the silhouette of Rachel in the dark. "Be careful," she whispered, closing the window.

Wow, I thought, *she called me "Wolf."* Was that good? Nobody much liked wolves. They were always coming down from the hills and killing livestock. But wolves were also strong and tough. Could it be she liked me? Twice now Rachel had helped me escape a beating — or worse. You didn't help someone you didn't like, did you?

Nate the Wolf, I thought. *Rachel's Wolf.* Wow! I felt like howling at the moon. I started strutting down the middle of Main Street.

"Nate," a voice behind me whispered. I whirled around. It was Josh.

"What are you doing here?" I asked.

"I got up to use the chamber pot, and I saw you creeping around. I was, shall we say, intrigued."

"Intrigued indeed," I muttered.

"I wondered what you were doing, and why you were doing it without me? But then I thought, he must like Rachel."

When I didn't respond, Josh laughed. "What'd you do, throw rocks at her window?"

"No."

"I'm proud of you, Nate. Mr. Shy and Bashful chasing the prettiest girl in Saybrook. What's got into you? It was risky, you know, with old man Pratt right there. He'd lop your head off if he caught you throwing rocks at his house. Boy, you must like her a lot."

We kept walking, and Josh kept chattering until he realized I was heading to the river, not the farm. "Where are you going, Nate? Love got you turned around?"

"I'm not in love."

"Uh-huh. So, to repeat the question, what are you doing? Why are you walking to the river in the middle of the night?"

I had to think about that one for a minute. I could lie and tell Josh I was night fishing with David and Ezra — that was what we'd agreed upon if someone asked. But Josh knew I hated fishing and besides, I didn't want to lie to my best friend. But yet I'd promised David I wouldn't tell anyone about the *Turtle*. I'd already broken that promise once with nearly disastrous results.

"I can't tell you," I said finally.

"Can't tell me!" Josh exclaimed. "Can't tell me? Of course you can. What's so important you can't tell your best friend?"

We were almost to the spot where the rowboat was hidden. I knew David and Ezra would be watching the shore for me. "Look, I'm sorry," I said, "but it's a secret. I promised. I've got to go."

Josh scowled and folded his arms across his chest. I felt his angry eyes boring into my back as I waded out to the boat. *Why did I ever agree to help build the submarine?* I asked myself, sighing. It had been nothing but trouble.

I heard voices in the distance, coming down the road toward us. "Who's that?" I whispered.

"Who cares?" Josh spat out angrily. "Maybe it's Mr. Pratt coming to get you for breaking Rachel's windows."

"I didn't break any windows. And I didn't throw anything, you fool! I was spying on him."

"Spying? Now we're getting somewhere. Why were you spying on Mr. Pratt?"

"I gotta go," I said, climbing into the boat.

"It *is* Pratt," Josh said. "I'd recognize that old bear's growl anywhere. Looks like Mr. Fenton, Mr. Smith, and Mr. Weatherbee, too. I wonder what they're doing out here?"

"Pratt? Oh my God! Get in the boat, Josh. If they find you here, they'll think you're working with me. They'll tar and feather you."

Josh started to protest, but the panic in my voice must have gotten his attention. He ran down the bank, tripped over a tree root, and fell face first into the water. I grabbed him by the collar and hauled him into the boat. Terrified, I tore the oars wildly toward the water, missed, and fell backward onto Josh's big belly. He let out a yelp.

I pulled myself up, grabbed the oars, and gave another mighty pull. This time the oars dug into the water, and we shot away from the bank. I rowed like a madman, and in just a few minutes we were halfway to the island.

"There they are," Josh whispered. Two lanterns had appeared on the bank. "Goodness, Nate, what did you do?"

I shook my head, gasping. Pain stabbed my sides. "No time now," I gasped.

Soon the lights on shore were just specks. "Nate, I thought you hated water. Suddenly you're a natural out here. What's going on?" Josh asked.

I was too worried to answer. We slid up to Poverty Island and I saw the comforting, familiar figure of Ezra wading out to us. As he pulled the rowboat to the little beach, I slumped over the oars, feeling like I might throw up. My arms, shoulders, and sides burned.

"I see we have company," Ezra said to me quietly, his eyes focusing on Josh.

"It couldn't be avoided," I gasped. "The Tories showed up."

"Tories?"

"It's not his fault I'm here," Josh said. "He was throwing rocks at Rachel Pratt's window, and I followed him, and we got chased."

"Why were you throwing rocks at Rachel Pratt's window?" Ezra asked.

Beginning to recover a little, I protested, "I *wasn't* throwing rocks at Rachel Pratt's window."

"David is going to be furious," Ezra said.

"It was Mr. Pratt," I said. "He and his pals are after the *Turtle*. I think they're coming to sink it."

Before Ezra could respond, David emerged from the trees. "Gentlemen, we're almost ready to go to New York," he said. Then he saw Josh. "What is *he* doing here?"

"There's no time to explain," Ezra said. "Pratt and his Tory friends are after the *Turtle*. We've got to move it now."

We hurried to the shed.

"What is that?" Josh asked, wide-eyed, staring at the *Turtle*. "Nate, tell me what's going on."

"It's a water machine," I said. "It goes underwater."

"Of course it does," Josh said, bewildered.

But there was no time to explain. We had to get out of there quickly. Using rope, we hauled the *Turtle* out to the water and attached it to the boat. "The sloop is waiting at the mouth of the river," David said. "You got here just in time, Nate."

We hurriedly launched out into the river. Ezra took the oars, and we moved downstream, tugging the heavy *Turtle* behind us.

"Don't look now, but we've got company," Josh said. Upstream, two lights were moving rapidly toward us.

Ezra rowed with all his might, but the lights quickly gained on us. In the moonlight I could see the outline of the men in the boat. There were four of them and four of us, but they were bigger and probably had guns.

"I should have stayed in bed," Josh groaned.

David was sitting in the stern, staring hard at our pursuers. Suddenly he stood up.

"Stop the boat, Ezra."

"Are you crazy? They'll sink the submarine, and who knows what they'll do to us."

"Ezra, get in the *Turtle*. It's time to go on the attack." It took a second, but Ezra understood. We opened the hatch on the conning tower and untied the ropes. Ezra squeezed his big body into the *Turtle* and closed the hatch. The craft quickly submerged until only the conning tower was visible. We watched as it moved upriver on a collision course with the Tories.

Mr. Pratt and company began pointing and shouting when they spied the *Turtle*. One of them lifted a musket and fired. *Sploosh!* The bullet splashed a few feet from the conning tower.

"Dive, Ezra, dive!" David shouted. As though Ezra could hear him, the conning tower disappeared almost immediately.

The astonished Tories stood in their boat, staring at the suddenly empty surface. "Where'd it go?" Mr. Pratt hollered.

The Tories were close, only fifty feet away. As they drifted nearer, they turned their attention from the water to us. "Looks like your chicken brother got away, but we've got you, Bushnell!" Mr. Pratt shouted. "How's the rotting belly of a British prison ship sound to you?"

The Tories pulled up beside us, leveling their muskets at our chests. "You too," Mr. Pratt snarled at me. "Don't think you can hide because you're a boy." He laughed. "I'll give Benjamin Franklin your new address in prison so he can write to you."

David glanced at the water, then at Pratt, eyes flashing defiantly. "Pratt, you're going to the bottom of the river."

"C'mon, let's take 'em in," Mr. Pratt said.

Suddenly the other Tories shouted in alarm. "Something's coming through the bottom of the boat!" one of them yelled.

I heard wood grinding and tearing. "It's a screw! That bastard in the water machine is trying to sink us!" another Tory screamed. A glittering metal screw was chewing a hole in the bottom of the Tories' boat. Then it withdrew and water poured in.

"Plug it, you idiots!" Pratt yelled. One of the men crouched, holding a piece of wood over the leak, but the boat was going down fast.

David nudged me with his foot. "Start rowing," he ordered. The current bore us quickly away from the sinking boat, and we halted a few hundred yards downstream. I glimpsed Mr. Pratt and his Tory pals swimming for shore.

"Looks like those rats will live to see another day," David said.

A few minutes later the *Turtle* surfaced nearby. The hatch opened and Ezra's head popped up.

"Wood screw?" David asked.

"Check," Ezra said with a big grin.

"Gentlemen, this was a good start," David said. "But we've got bigger boats to attack: British men-o-war. Tomorrow we go to New York."

Exasperated, Josh gave me a puzzled look, and I nodded. I knew I had a lot of explaining to do.

Chapter 8

As much as he wanted to be a part of our plan, Josh knew it would be too risky for him to come to New York. We said our goodbyes, and I joined Ezra and David on the sloop we'd borrowed from a shipyard in Saybrook. A small crew did the sailing, leaving us to ourselves.

The voyage to New York was the longest two weeks of my life. We were on the water all day long, no stops and no getting off. At night we anchored in little coves, the waves rocking the boat, reminding me all night long that we were on the water. I got so worn out worrying about something bad happening, like the sloop sinking or me falling overboard, I started to get sick.

"We're going to get to New York whether you worry about it or not," Ezra said to me one day. "You might as well relax and enjoy the journey."

I was too tired to argue, so I sat down next to him. Ezra was doing what he'd done every day since we'd sailed from Saybrook: staring at the sea and napping in the sun. David was nearby, tinkering with the *Turtle*, which was tied down to the deck.

"Nate, maybe you should try my approach," Ezra said. "When I've got something worrying me, I always ask myself, 'What's the worst thing that could happen?'" He looked at me. "With us being out on the water, what's the worst thing that could happen?"

"The sloop could sink, and I'd drown," I said without a moment's hesitation.

"What would happen to you if the sloop sinks and you drown?"

I thought for a moment. "I'd die."

"Would that be so bad?"

According to everything I'd heard in church, I would go to heaven after I died. It was supposed to be a wonderful place, something to look forward to. Still, like the murky waters surrounding us, heaven was a great wide unknown.

"I guess not," I replied, only half-assured.

"All right then. Now relax, and every time you start to feel afraid, remember the worst thing that can happen."

For the next week I followed Ezra's example and did a whole lot of nothing. Every day I sat by his side staring at the water. When he napped, I napped. When I felt afraid, I tried to think about going to heaven. And a funny thing happened. After a while, the ocean didn't seem so forbidding. I wasn't about to dive in and go swimming, but the fear didn't seem so strong, like it could swallow me alive.

At the end of the two weeks, the sloop deposited the *Turtle* and the three of us in a little cove on York Island, northeast of the city. And I had survived.

"There's no wagon," David grumbled. "I sent a message to General Putnam telling him when and where to meet us."

"Don't worry, big brother," Ezra said. "Israel Putnam is a Connecticut man like us. He's not going to let us down, especially since we're bringing a secret weapon."

Sure enough, a few hours later a cart with two horses rolled up. The droopy-eyed driver gazed out at us from under a large felt hat. David walked over and extended his right hand. "I'm David Bushnell from Connecticut."

The man ignored David's hand. "Corporal Allen," he said. He shot a contemptuous glance at the *Turtle*. "This is the famous water machine from Connecticut? Don't look like much."

There was an awkward silence. "It's called the *American Turtle*," I said helpfully. "Because it looks like a turtle. At least, it looked like a turtle when we first started." I faltered as the corporal glared at me. "Well, uh, the two halves looked like turtle shells . . . before we sealed them together."

"Uh-huh," Corporal Allen grunted. "There's thirty thousand British and Hessian reg'lars over on Staten Island, and they send us a turtle. God Almighty help us."

After another long silence David asked, "How'd you know about the, uh, water machine?"

"Know? Everyone knows. It's all over camp."

David, Ezra, and I exchanged puzzled looks. "I guess it doesn't matter, as long as the British don't know," David said.

Corporal Allen chuckled. "Even if they knew, Mr. — what'd ya say — Bush? Even if they knew they wouldn't be scared a' *that*," he said, jerking a thumb at the *Turtle*. "And I *know* Black Dick ain't gonna be scared of no turtle."

"Black Dick? Who's that?" I asked.

"He's admiral of the whole British fleet. Admiral Richard Howe. His men call him Black Dick because he's so tough," Allen said.

Soon we were jolting south toward New York City.

David and Ezra had insisted I sit up front with Corporal Allen while they held the *Turtle* steady. At first I was pleased with this privilege, but I soon found out why they wanted to sit in the back: Corporal Allen stank to high heaven.

After about an hour, we topped a rise and I saw the city in the distance. Houses and buildings filled the land leading down to the harbor. It looked like a thousand Saybrooks packed together. "Ezra, David, look," I said, pointing.

Corporal Allen grunted. "You think that's something, wait 'til you see the ships."

"Oh, I've seen ships," I said. "I'm from New London."

Corporal Allen seemed unimpressed. "Just wait, boy."

A few minutes later I saw what he meant. Across the water, warships of all sizes crowded the harbor. Hundreds of masts pierced the sky. "Oh my," Ezra said quietly. "It looks like a pine forest with all the limbs cut off."

"You see why your water machine is folly?" muttered Corporal Allen. "What can you do against so many?"

David's eyes blazed. "We'll do what we can do," he said, turning toward Ezra and me. "What I see are targets, gentlemen, hundreds of targets."

I was inclined to agree with the corporal, but I kept my mouth shut. Who did we think we were? I remembered Uncle Elias's words the night David had spread out the plan for the submarine: *"David, only you would dream of taking on the biggest navy in the world with a science project."*

"Can you tell me where General Washington is?" David asked Corporal Allen.

"The general? Down in the city where headquarters is. He goes back and forth between the city and Long Island. He's got half the army here and half over there. I guess he ain't real sure where General Howe — that's Black Dick's brother — is going to attack first. Guess our little rebellion has got England's attention. They got both Howes here, the general and the admiral."

He shook his head. "There's too much territory to defend, too many rivers and harbors and such. With all those ships and men, they can come at us wherever they want. It's like General Washington is trying to plug a hundred leaks with only ten fingers." Corporal Allen chortled and held up his left hand. It had only two fingers and the thumb. "Course, some of us got more fingers to plug holes with than others."

As we neared the city, military activity grew. Companies of soldiers marched past. The uniforms varied wildly, from buckskin to well-tailored blue outfits. In some of the units the men slouched along, looking around aimlessly. Others kept good order and marched in unison, heads held high.

We rolled all the way through the city until we ran out

of land. A group of soldiers stood around several cannon pointed toward the harbor. We got a lot of strange looks when they saw the *Turtle*.

One soldier broke away from the group and strode up to us. "This must be the famous water machine from Connecticut," he said. "Welcome to Whitehall Battery."

"Have you been expecting us?" David asked.

"Well, you never know what to believe around here. There's a new rumor every day. But they said Benjamin Franklin was the one talking about the water machine, so I believed it."

"Well, it's true," David said, smiling at me. "You might say Dr. Franklin is a friend of mine. Would you and some of the other men be willing to help us get the water machine in the, uh, water?"

Soon the *Turtle* was tethered to a nearby dock. It was hard to believe we were finally in New York, within striking distance of the British. I gazed across the harbor to the warships in the distance. Ezra would be out amongst them in the *Turtle,* planting the bomb. David would supervise the attack. And me, what would I do?

That's what Uncle Elias had wondered when David asked him if I could come to New York.

"What do you need Nathan for? The submarine is built and you've got Ezra."

"I don't have a good answer, Elias," David had replied.

"I've just got this feeling we're going to need him before everything is said and done."

Uncle Elias had tugged on his beard. "I'm sorry, David, but a feeling isn't a good enough reason to send a boy to war . . . especially without his father's permission. What if something happens to him?"

"That's exactly what I'm thinking, Elias, but for a different reason. I'm thinking, what if something *good* happens to Nate because he goes to New York? I think his father would understand that."

"Something good? What good could come out of sending a boy to war? He could get killed."

"That's true, Elias. Anything can happen in war. He could get killed. Or he could end up doing something he'll be proud of. The point is, Nate will never know if he stays here."

Elias sighed, shook his head, and looked at me. "Nate, what do you want to do?"

To be honest, I didn't know. I was scared to stay and scared to go. If I went, I'd be in a war and who knew what terrible thing could happen? If I stayed, I'd be in a war with myself — always wondering what I might have done for the Revolution.

"I guess I'll go," I finally said.

"All right," Elias said reluctantly. "But David, don't let him out of your sight."

So there I was in New York, wondering what the heck I was supposed to do. Thoughts of Papa kept popping into my head. I'd been so busy with the *Turtle* and running from Butch all summer, I hadn't thought much about Papa. But now that he was so close, maybe just down one of these streets with his regiment, I couldn't stop thinking about him. The soldiers were saying a battle would happen soon. What if Papa got killed or captured? I might never see him again.

I tossed about trying to sleep that night in a tent some soldiers had loaned us. David woke me up. "Nate, what's the matter? You've kicked me three times."

I could just make out David's face in the moonlight that slipped in through the tent flap. "It's Papa," I whispered. "I want to see him."

"So that's your nightmare? Your father?"

"What if something happens to him?"

"What if something *doesn't* happen to him?"

Ezra had stirred awake. "Nate, remember what you're supposed to do when you're worried?" he asked sleepily. "What's the worst thing that could happen?"

"Papa could get killed," I hesitated. ". . . and go to heaven."

"Would that be so bad?"

"Well, not for him. But it wouldn't be so good for me."

David sighed. "Nate, New York is huge. There are

thousands of soldiers here. We'll never find him. Besides, we've got so much to do. We've got to meet with General Putnam to plan the *Turtle*'s first attack. We need to study the currents in the harbor. We need to get the bomb ready. We don't have time to look for your father."

"You don't need me for all that, David. You've got Ezra." I paused. "All I've got is Papa."

I couldn't be sure in the dark, but I'd swear David's eyes teared up a little. We sat quietly for a minute or two.

"You're right, Nate. You've already lost your mother, and you've only got one father," David finally said. "I remember when my father died out in the field that day. He was there in the morning and in the afternoon he wasn't. . . . I wished I'd had a chance to say goodbye."

David sighed again. "I still want you to be around to help with the *Turtle*, but really there's nothing that Ezra and I can't handle ourselves. Go find your father, but don't go too far. I want to know where you are."

Then David smiled. "But if you ever tell Elias I let you out of my sight, I'll whack you one."

* * *

The following morning I was walking the streets of New York, marveling at the many fortifications. The city bristled with barricades and batteries of cannon. Every street corner seemed to have a guard.

"Do you know where the Seventh Connecticut Volunteers are?" I asked soldier after soldier. No one knew. Hours later, as I was rounding a corner I heard a sweet sound: soldiers with Connecticut accents.

"You from Connecticut?" I asked them.

"Milford," a young-looking man said. "You?"

"New London."

We looked at each other awkwardly for a few moments. Finally the Milford man asked, "What is a New London boy doing here? Why aren't you home fishing?"

I decided to show off. "I'm here with the water machine."

"The water machine? I heard about that. They say it's got a cannon mounted on the top."

"Well, not exactly, but it *is* dangerous."

"Hope so. We've got our hands full with about the whole British fleet here."

"You know where the Seventh Connecticut Volunteers are?"

"I do," said one of the other soldiers. "I've got a cousin with 'em. They're over on the Brooklyn Heights across the river, working on one of the forts."

"Do you know how can I get over there?" I asked.

"You can't," said the soldier. "Not unless you're on army business."

"Why don't you take your water machine across?" asked the young man from Milford.

I shook my head. "It's already on army business." An older, grizzled soldier shrugged. "Heck, why don't you join up with us? We're supposed to go over to Long Island soon. We're the Third Company of the Fifth Connecticut."

When I didn't respond, he grinned. "It ain't like everyone here is of legal age," he said, jostling the Milford man with his elbow.

"You be quiet," the young man retorted.

"Oh, don't fret, Joe. No one is going to kick you out of the army now, with a fight coming on."

The younger man laughed and extended his hand toward me. "I'm Joe Martin and I'm — " he looked exaggeratedly from side to side, "fifteen. But let's keep that between the three of us."

I shook his hand, delighted with his confession. "I'm Nathan Wade and I'm *almost* fifteen." My birthday was three months away.

"So why do you want to go over to the island?" Joe asked.

"I'm looking for my father," I said. "He's with the Seventh."

Joe nodded solemnly. "You're not going over unless you're a soldier or a strong swimmer."

I winced.

"C'mon, Nathan, I'll show you around," he said. "It'd be nice to have someone my age to talk to for a while."

We walked down the street to a huge brick house. "We're staying here," Joe said. "Used to be some fancy Tory's house, so we requisitioned it. There's a lot of Tories in New York. At least until we showed up."

It was the biggest house I'd ever seen. I'd swear all of Saybrook could fit inside, with the Bushnell farm thrown in to boot.

"There's a nice view of Long Island from the roof," Joe said. "Wanna have a look?"

A few minutes later we stepped outside an upstairs window onto the roof. Seagulls dove in the river far below, snapping up fish. Boats loaded with soldiers rowed across, oars dipping in and out of the water.

"See the man over on the Heights?" Joe asked. A tiny figure on a platform waved miniature flags. "He's the signalman. He's sending messages for the army on the island to the other army over here."

"What's he saying?" I asked.

Joe shrugged. "You got me. *Send reinforcements, we're about to be attacked!* Or *Lunch was lousy. What's for dinner?*"

We sat and enjoyed the view. It was so beautiful I could hardly imagine a battle was about to break out somewhere below us.

"So what do you think, Nathan?" he asked. "You want to join up with us? Or do they need you back with the water machine?"

"Naw, the water machine is ready. They don't need me. I just want to see my father, that's all. I didn't come to fight."

Joe thought for a minute. "You sure?"

I looked at Joe, startled. "Sure about what?"

"Sure you didn't come to fight? I think it's fine you wanting to see your pa, and I hope you find him. But if you're done with the water machine, maybe there's something else you can do for the cause, like fight."

When Joe said "fight," I think I winced again, like when he had mentioned swimming.

"Was your pa proud of you when you joined up?" I asked.

Joe laughed. "He didn't know I was doing it, so I can't say for sure. I made my mark on the papers when the recruiters came to Milford. They marched me off before my pa had the chance to find out."

"Didn't they ask how old you were?"

Joe shook his head. "I'm big for my age, like you. They must have figured I was old enough. Or maybe they just needed men bad and took whoever they could get."

We watched the river in silence for a few minutes. "You know, Nathan," Joe said. "I didn't join up to impress my pa or anyone else. I did it for myself and for my country, pure and simple."

He looked at me. "If you decide to join, that's why you should do it. Personally, I think you'd be a fine soldier."

I felt a thrill run down my spine, just like when David asked me to help build the submarine. "Me?" I said. "I don't think I'm brave enough."

"Well, between you and me, *I'm* scared." He nodded toward the soldiers on the street. "Probably everyone down there is afraid too, not that any of them are going to say it. One thing I've learned is soldiers don't talk about being afraid to fight or dying in battle."

"Are you scared you might die?"

"I don't think about it. If I did, I'd probably run like a rabbit. You want to know what I'm most afraid of? I'm afraid I'll run as soon as the shooting starts and let the other men in the regiment down."

"So if you don't *feel* brave, how do you *be* brave?" I asked.

We watched boats full of soldiers crossing the river. "My pa once told me that real courage isn't not feeling afraid. If you weren't afraid, you wouldn't need courage, right? He says courage is doing the right thing, even when you're scared to death."

Joe's face stiffened with resolve. "That's what I've

decided to do," he said. "I'm going to do my duty as best I can and leave the outcome with Providence."

There was something strong in Joe's face — something I wanted for myself. *What was the right thing to do?* I wondered. Look for Papa? Go back to David and Ezra? Join the army? My brain was spinning with choices.

I thought about Joe's words: if you join up, do it for yourself and for your country. Maybe joining up was the "something good" David thought could happen to me here. How could I know for sure?

"I'm going with you," I burst out. I didn't feel entirely sure, but I felt like I did when I'd leveled Butch Hyde with my legs: I couldn't believe what I'd done.

Joe's face broke into a grin. "C'mon, I'll take you down to meet the other men."

*　　*　　*

That night I ate supper with the rest of the company. The sergeant said he'd sign me up officially the next day and try to find me a uniform. I decided I'd write David a letter in the morning, telling him my plans.

I slept on a hallway floor on top of a plush rug. The next morning I woke to the rumble of distant thunder. All around me, heads popped out of blankets.

"Sounds like the shooting has started on Long Island," someone said.

A wave of fear passed over me. We pulled on our hats and boots and hurried outside. The sun was rising, huge, red, and angry.

"Fall in!" shouted an officer. "March!"

I fell into a line of soldiers, feeling out of place with no uniform or musket, marching as best I could. When the men were "lefting" with their feet, I was "righting," but it didn't seem to matter. Joe sensed my discomfort.

"We've only been together a few months, so it isn't like you've got much catching up to do," he said.

As we marched along, I remembered the letter I had meant to write to David. It would have to wait until later. Crowds of people cheered as we went by, shouting, "Get those lobsterbacks, boys!" At the ferry the company narrowed into single file to descend the steps to the river. Two large casks filled with biscuits stood at the top of the stairs.

"It's sea bread," Joe said. "Better getcha some. One thing I've learned about soldiering is that you always eat as much as you can whenever you can. You don't always know when you'll eat next."

I stuffed my pockets with the small biscuits. I bit one and winced. "We smash 'em up with cannonballs," Joe said. "It's the only way. Teeth aren't hard enough."

As we descended the steps to the landing below, I felt another jolt of fear. The water was a good mile across.

Water, water everywhere. Why was I never able to get away from it?

Hundreds of people had gathered, cheering as each boatload of soldiers launched. I followed Joe aboard a long flatboat. Men in neat white pants and blue jackets manned the oars. I sat down next to one of the sailors, who nodded at me. As we pushed away from the landing, one of the officers shouted, "Three cheers for America, men!"

"Hurrah!" the soldiers shouted, punching their muskets heavenward. "Hurrah! Hurrah!" The crowd roared three cheers back. A thrill ran through me, and for a moment I forgot my fear. What a great adventure! I was miles and miles from home. And I was a soldier in the Continental Army.

The thrill, however, ebbed as we neared Long Island. The roar of cannon grew louder. The smell of sulfur hung heavy in the air, and my mouth went dry. I could see frantic activity on the Brooklyn ferry. Men were unloading boats and equipment, and their distant shouts carried across the water. I focused on the soft grunts of the sailors as they dipped the oars into the water and anxiously watched the shore.

The low voice of the sailor next to me interrupted my thoughts. "You're our fifth load today," he said. "Looks like they got quite a battle going on. We'd like to be fighting, but they got us rowing." He sighed. "Guess we're too good with boats. We're Marbleheaders, a slew of fishermen."

Marblehead was a fishing town up the coast from New London in Massachusetts. "I'm from New London," I said.

"All of you?" the man asked. "We could use some more seamen to help ferry men over."

"No. The rest of them are from western Connecticut. I just joined up."

"I was wondering why you didn't have a gun or a uniform." He dipped the oar in the water and pulled back in perfect unison with the other sailors. "So we got us a load of farmers and tanners and blacksmiths. Well, as long as they can shoot, I guess it doesn't matter."

He glanced at me. "You've got a fisherman's arms, boy. If you can't find a gun, come and find me. I'll find you an oar."

Soon we were marching up a road away from the ferry. To our left was the Heights. The steep hill was crowned with several forts and long earthen walls, and I saw hundreds of soldiers watching the battle below.

The bellow of muskets and cannon grew louder. We hadn't gone far when we began to see bloodied soldiers. One held his cheek like he was trying to keep it from falling off his face. Another with a bloody leg limped along, using his musket for a crutch. Other men didn't appear to be wounded, just dazed.

"What's it like? Is it a hard fight?" one of our men asked a filthy soldier sitting by the side of the road. The man stared straight ahead with a vacant expression and said nothing.

Farther up the road we came upon a group of men trying to haul a stuck cannon out of the sandy soil. "Hey, help us out, will you?" one of the artillerymen begged.

But an officer ordered us onward. "There's a battle on, boys!" he yelled. A few hundred yards ahead was a large swampy area, a creek the tide had flowed into from the nearby harbor. Beyond, small figures rushed back and forth amid great clouds of smoke. The ground trembled from the cannon and musket fire.

"The double quick, boys, the double quick!" the officer shouted.

The regiment surged forward in a fast trot. I loped along, gun-less and gasping, wondering what madness I had thrust myself into. *You fool!* I said to myself. Why hadn't I stayed with David? We pulled up next to the water, unable to move forward. The swamp was about eighty yards across, and a strong current coursed through it. In the distance I could see a thin line of scarlet uniforms standing against a sea of the enemy. More British and Hessian troops were rushing up. Rallied by an officer waving a sword, the scarlet line charged. In the thick, clinging smoke, men swirled in a wild melee. Musket flashes

93

stabbed the air. Men crumpled to the earth. Screams and curses filled my ears. The roar was deafening, and I stood dumbstruck.

The scarlet line fell back to its original place. Again the officer rallied them, and again they charged the enemy. "Good God! It's Lord Stirling and the Marylanders! I recognize the uniforms!" the officer shouted. "They're fighting like wolves!"

My mind went to the night Rachel Pratt caught me outside her window and called me "Wolf." I had nothing in common with the sharp-toothed and fearless beast. *A mouse is more like it,* I thought. *I'm like a mouse trying to avoid a trap.*

Soon only a handful of the Maryland men were clumped around Stirling, who still defiantly waved his sword at the enemy.

"They're covering the retreat!" Joe exclaimed.

Stampeding like a herd of wild cattle, the routed Continental Army headed toward the water. Hundreds of soldiers had plunged into the swamp. Some were mired in the mud and screamed for help. I watched in horror as soldiers sank and did not come back up. Wild with fear, others swam desperately toward us.

Redcoats suddenly appeared on the shore, and two cannons began blasting grapeshot at the swimming soldiers.

"Bastards!" Joe shouted.

The men we'd passed on the road pulled up alongside us. They quickly loaded the cannon and began blazing back at the British. As the swimming soldiers got closer, some of the men in Third Company waded out to help them ashore. I stared, stricken with fear. I knew I should help, but I couldn't step into the water. I was afraid I'd drown.

Muddy, bloody, and sopping wet, the survivors stumbled ashore. Some knelt, gasping for breath. Others looked about frantically in terror. A few wept like injured children.

Suddenly one soldier splashed ashore, brushed past me, and kept on going. Something inside me snapped, and I ran after him. I didn't care if anyone saw me, even Joe. I just knew I couldn't be there anymore. I ran after the wet, barefoot soldier. All around us hundreds of men were running.

We ran together, seeking the safety of the Heights.

Chapter 9

Rain was running off my hat and down my neck. A nor'easter had blown in the day after the battle. One long, rain-soaked day and night had gone by, and it was still pounding down late the next afternoon. The water in the trench I stood in had risen to my thighs.

"Another beautiful day in Brooklyn," muttered the soldier next to me, whom I secretly called the Grumbler. I didn't nod or respond. I simply stood there soaked and miserable, wondering what I should do.

Brooklyn Heights seemed safe enough. Thousands of soldiers were positioned behind thick walls of earth and logs. Small forts bristling with cannons rose above the earthworks. Tangled thickets and forests choked all approaches to the Heights, except for a "kill zone" the men had cleared — one hundred feet of open space to repel any redcoats foolish enough to attack up the slope.

Despite these defenses, I'd barely slept. I don't think anyone had. The rain pounded down hour after hour without letting up. Worse, I feared the attack that the soldiers around me said could happen at any minute. Everyone kept squinting over the earthworks toward the enemy lines. About five hundred yards away, redcoats were busy digging trenches, inching like ants ever closer to our lines.

Why they hadn't attacked, no one knew. "The lobsterbacks would have bagged the lot of us if they hadn't stopped," Grumbler said.

"It's all uphill," said a soldier I called the Mumbler. "We'd slaughter 'em all the way up. They're afraid it would be Bunker Hill all over again. That's why they're digging siege trenches."

"Slaughter 'em?" Grumbler snapped. "Slaughter 'em? With wet powder?"

It was true. Along our little part of the line, most of our muskets were worthless.

"I heard some idiot forgot to cover the wagons carrying

97

all the gunpowder," Grumbler said. "If the British attack, all you'll hear from us is one big click."

"Then they'll level their bayonets and charge, and that will be the end of us," Mumbler said. "We don't have any powder, and we don't have any bayonets. How are we supposed to fight?"

No one asked me questions, which was fine. Maybe it's because I finally had a gun, and they thought I was one of them. I'd seen a musket and an empty powderhorn lying in the road during the panicked retreat to the Heights, and somehow I'd had the sense to pick it up. I had no musket balls or gunpowder, but the thick wood felt good in my hands.

The gun was the only thing that felt good. As dark descended for the third night since the battle, I shivered and wondered what to do. I could try to get back across the river to the city, but they might think I was a deserter — and deserters got shot. Or I could try to find Joe and the rest of the company — after I'd run like a coward. Or I could stay put — and wait for a bayonet assault. *I'm doomed no matter what I do,* I thought.

Or I could look for Papa. He might be down on the battlefield, dead, but he might be alive. He'd be furious to see me so far from Saybrook, but at least he could tell me what to do.

When it was dark, I eased out of the trench and began

slogging my way down the line. Here and there men were able to keep campfires going under makeshift canvas shelters.

I stuck my head inside one of these tents. "Any of you seen Joshua Wade of the Seventh Connecticut Volunteers?" I asked. Eyes flicked toward my face. Some men didn't look at all, staring blankly into the pathetic little fire. Finally one of the men shook his head. "No, boy."

I worked my way down the line, getting the same answer from group after group. "Sorry son, there were hundreds killed and captured," said one soldier. "He might be down on the battlefield somewheres."

I'd never felt lonelier in my life. The rain beat down mercilessly on my face and back as I walked a dark stretch of the line. Shivers shook my shoulders and arms. I was ready to curl up in a hole and wait for some redcoat to run me through with his bayonet.

About fifty yards ahead a fire pricked the darkness. *One more*, I thought. *I'll ask one more time if they've seen Papa, and then I'll find my hole.* Five men were huddled around a small fire under some coats they'd balanced on their muskets. "Anyone here seen Joshua Wade of the Seventh Connecticut Volunteers?"

A man whose face was hooded by a blanket turned toward me. "Nathan Wade, is that you?" he asked.

Crickey, it was Butch Hyde! "Butch? What are you

99

doing here?" I realized it was a stupid question as soon as I blurted it out. *You fool, why do you think he's here? For fun?*

Butch pulled the blanket down to his shoulders. "Come out of the rain, Wade." The other men glanced at Butch and shifted to make room. I sat on my haunches in front of him, my rear an inch above a muddy puddle. Wet strands of hair were plastered across my forehead and face.

Butch looked tired and worn. In the flickering firelight, I glimpsed an angry red gouge that ran halfway across his forehead. I was so glad to see someone I knew that I didn't care if he was my archenemy.

"Did you see my mama before you left Saybrook?" Butch asked.

"No, we had to leave fast."

Butch nodded and squinted at the fire, eyes moist.

"I came down with David and Ezra. . . . We built a water machine to attack the British ships in the harbor," I said.

Butch grunted. "I heard something about that. I guess I should have figured it was Bushnell when they said it came from Connecticut. He was always one to tinker with things."

"Have you seen my father?" I asked.

"Not since before the battle. We were on the Old Jamaica Road, and about ten thousand redcoats got in our rear. We never saw 'em coming. It got pretty hot. We held out for a while, but there were too many of them."

Butch must have noticed my long face. "He's probably all right, Wade. A lot of men got scattered from their regiments during the fight. He's probably down the line somewhere."

"How's your father?"

Butch looked away. "Not too good. He took a ball in the shoulder. I got him to the rear. We barely got away from their bayonets. That's where I got this," he pointed to the cut on his forehead. "They took Pa across the river to the city." He sighed deeply. "I had to stay here — duty, you know."

Suddenly I remembered what I'd said to Josh back in Saybrook: *"I hope Butch Hyde gets killed by the British."* My cheeks flushed with regret. I couldn't believe I'd said something so ugly! The bullying in Saybrook seemed a thousand miles away, almost like it didn't happen. This tired, bloodied Butch didn't seem so bad.

We sat watching the rain, two boys in the middle of a war, worried about our fathers. I knew I needed to keep looking for Papa, but I lingered, reluctant to give up Butch's company. Finally I stood up. "Good-bye, Butch," I said. "I'm going to keep looking for Papa."

Butch stood up. "I hate to see you go. But that's what I'd do if I was you." He extended his hand toward me.

Memories of all the humiliation I'd suffered from Butch flooded back. The taunts, the shoves, and the fear I'd felt for so many summers crowded into my mind, clamoring for revenge. The old, familiar hatred seized me. *Shake his hand? Never!*

I was about to whirl around and stomp off, leaving his unshaken hand hanging. That would show him. I sensed a nudge within, from Providence perhaps, telling me to let go of my anger. But Butch had hurt me, I argued; he'd done me wrong for no reason at all.

For the longest second of my life I agonized. Then, I stuck out my hand. I gripped Butch's hand firmly and looked him square in the eyes. I couldn't believe what I said next: "Butch, I'm sorry for hating you all this time. It wasn't right."

Butch blinked in surprise. "I don't know that you're the one who needs to be sorry, Wade. I'm the one . . ."

I cut him off. "It doesn't matter."

Butch shook his head. "Heck, I was scared that some-day you'd stand up for yourself. As big as you are, you could've whipped me. You finally did — knocked me down in front of Rachel Pratt. Remember? I was so mad." He laughed, a deep belly laugh that sounded strangely out of place in the gloomy trenches. The soldiers sitting in the tent looked at us like we were crazy.

I laughed too. "Yeah, I can't believe I did that." I lingered, savoring the moment. "Well, I need to go. You take care, Butch."

As I walked away Butch called out, "Hey Nathan! Good luck with that water machine. Sink some ships for us, all right?"

"All right, Butch. You shoot us some redcoats."

I began working my way down the line again, asking for Papa. It was the same as before: "I ain't heard of him." But I also heard men talking desertion. "As soon as the rain stops, the lobsterbacks will be on us," one soldier said. "That fool Washington has got us trapped between the redcoats and the river. If this nor'easter didn't have their fleet bottled up in the harbor, those boats would be in our rear so quick we'd be blown to bits. There's no way out."

No way out. I imagined bayonets stabbing and thrusting at my guts. The morning light would bring row upon row of redcoats from the trenches a few hundred yards away. With parade-ground precision, they would level their deadly steel and charge.

I tried to push the fear from my mind, but it just grew. By the time I'd worked most of the way down the line, I was so nervous I felt like throwing up. Men stood every ten feet or so in the flooded trench, staring toward the British lines.

My legs numb, I stopped. Cold water splashed around my knees as I stepped down into the trench and took a place in the line. The soldier to my right nodded, and I nodded back. A few minutes later he waded over.

"Have you noticed?" he asked.

"Noticed what?"

"Since midnight they've been pulling regiments out of the line and spreading the rest of us out right and left. The line is getting mighty thin. I don't know if we're retreating or getting ready to attack."

"I don't know either," I said. "I'm just looking for my father." The soldier didn't seem to hear me and returned to his post.

Sure enough, a half hour later we were ordered to shift to the right. The soldier to my right was now thirty feet away. A little later, we shifted to the right again. The man to my right was now fifty feet away.

Around two in the morning, the order came for us to move out. We lined up and began trotting rearward. "Think we're evacuating?" I asked one man.

"Lord, I hope so," he said.

An officer ran over, furious. "Silence!" he hissed. "Our orders are absolute silence! If the enemy hears us moving out, they'll slaughter us like cattle." Chastened, we stole rearward, quiet as cats. We quickened our pace when we reached the road to the ferry. *We're retreating!* I exulted. *We're getting out of here!*

Darkness shrouded the ferry. In the moonlight, hundreds of soldiers stood waiting. Officers on horseback moved about, keeping order and issuing quiet commands. Beyond them, small boats dotted the East River — longboats, whaleboats, sailboats.

Loud shouting broke the calm. A group of soldiers was trying to force their way onto a crowded boat. A tall officer rode up, swung down from his mount, and pushed his way over to them. He picked up a large rock and held it over the boat.

"Get off, or I'll sink this boat to hell!" he shouted. The rebellious men backed away. A vast, respectful silence filled the area around the ferry. The evacuation resumed.

"That was General Washington," the man in front of me whispered. "He'd have sunk it, too."

The crowd in front of us slowly shrank as the boats continued their endless two-mile round trips between Long Island and New York. General Washington rode up to several officers standing near us.

"Good God, General Mifflin! I would not have expected you to abandon your post," Washington exclaimed.

"Sir, we didn't abandon our post. I did it by your order," General Mifflin replied.

"It can't be."

"By God, I did. Did Scammell act as your aide for the day, or did he not?"

"He did."

"There you are!" Mifflin said. "I got the order through him."

Washington frowned and shook his head. "It was a dreadful mistake. You must return immediately to your posts. We will have terrible consequences if the enemy sees we aren't there."

My heart sank. Back to the trenches? Filled with dread, I slunk back to the earthworks with the rest of the regiment. In the distance were the silhouettes of the British sentries. They didn't seem to have noticed our absence.

The dark edge of the eastern horizon was softening. *Dawn was coming, and death would not be far behind,* I thought in despair. The rain was slackening. When the storm ended the British would attack. We weren't going to be saved after all. There simply wasn't enough time.

"Hey!" a voice hissed. A soldier standing about thirty feet to my right was waving me over. As I walked toward him he turned to his right and waved another soldier over. We stood on a muddy patch of grass above the trench. The man who had waved me over was short and wore tattered buckskin. The other soldier was about my height, with piercing blue eyes and long ragged hair.

The short man looked up at us and asked shyly, "Do either of you fellas know the part of the Bible about the shepherd and the valley?" He looked over at the British lines. "I'm thinking we need some help pretty dang quick.

The rain is easing up, and once it quits, they'll be comin' over."

The blue-eyed man considered this for a moment. "The twenty-third Psalm," he said finally. "I know it . . . or how it starts anyway."

"If you can get it started, it might spark my memory," said the short man. He looked at me. "How about you?"

To be honest, I couldn't remember a bit of it. In church I'd heard all the Psalms and a bunch more of the Bible, and on Sunday afternoons when I was little Papa had read the Scriptures to us. But I felt so crushed down with fear I could barely breathe, much less remember something about a shepherd. "I think I could manage a bit of it," I said.

"Here goes then," said the blue-eyed man. "The Lord is my shepherd; I shall not want. He maketh me to lie down in green pastures: he leadeth me beside the still waters." He looked into the distance like he was looking for the words, and shrugged. "That's all I remember."

The short man picked up where the blue-eyed man had left off. "He restoreth my soul: he leadeth me in the paths of righteousness for his name's sake. Yea . . . Yea . . . Yea . . ."

"Yea, though I walk," said the blue-eyed man.

"Yea!" exclaimed the short man. "Yea, though I walk through the valley of the shadow of death . . . though I walk through the valley of the shadow of death . . . though I walk through the dadgum valley of the shadow of death. . . . I don't remember any more."

The two men looked at me expectantly. I was staring at my boots, locked up with fear. I closed my eyes and rocked back and forth a bit. *Providence, please help me remember!*

Suddenly words popped into my mind. "I will fear no evil," I said quietly, "for thou art with me; thy rod and thy staff they comfort me."

"Yup, there you go," said the short man.

"Thou preparest a table before me in the presence of mine enemies: thou anointest my head with oil; my cup runneth over. Surely goodness and mercy shall follow me all the days of my life: and I will dwell in the house of the Lord forever."

I opened my eyes. "That's all I remember."

"I think that's all there is," the blue-eyed man said.

The rain had ended. It was light enough to see the distant outlines of the British fortifications. An officer was walking our line, giving instructions. "Men, if you've got any dry powder, charge your weapon," he said. "If the redcoats come, aim low. Make them pay for every step."

"Son, let me charge your gun," the short man said. "I stashed some powder that didn't get wet." After he'd loaded my gun, I walked back toward my spot on the line. I felt strangely calm. *Let the redcoats come. I'll get off a shot and then . . .* I decided not to think about it.

Before I stepped into the trench, I glanced down at my boots. Strange, I couldn't see them. They were covered in . . . cotton? I looked around the earthworks. My goodness, I realized with a start, it was fog. A dense, molasses-thick fog was rising off the ground. Great and wonderful, billowy masses of fog! *Fog! Fog! Fog!* In minutes the air was so white I couldn't see five feet in front of me.

The short soldier was cackling. "Hey, boys!" he hollered. "Looks like we're going to get off this island after all. The redcoats can't attack through this!"

I curled up in the cold mud and basked in the luxuriant, white cloud like it was a thick, warm blanket. For the first time in three days I fell sound asleep. I dreamt I was in the loft at the Bushnell's, Ezra's familiar snore beside me. I pulled the blanket over my head and was drifting off to sleep when I heard the *splat, splat* of horse hooves on mud outside the house.

Then the most beautiful words I'd ever heard passed through the blanket into my ears: "Regiment, prepare to move out."

Chapter 10

Thick fog hung over the ferry. The area around the landing was much less crowded than it had been during our first trip in the middle of the night. Small groups of soldiers stood staring at the water. Suddenly a longboat eased out of the mist and pulled up to the ferry. I climbed on board with several dozen other men.

"I see you finally found a gun," a voice whispered.

I looked down and saw the same sailor I'd talked to on the trip over three days earlier. "Oh, this," I muttered, looking at my musket. I'd gotten so used to carrying it, I'd forgotten I even had it.

"I heard it was quite a fight."

"Yes sir, it was." I hoped he didn't want details. I wasn't eager to revisit my memories of the bloodbath in the pond or my panicked flight to the Heights.

"Wished we could've been there. Our regiment came over as reinforcements yesterday, and I thought sure we were going to fight." He shrugged. "They're saying it's a lucky thing we came over. General Washington ordered every boat for five miles around gathered up; then they put us to work around midnight. We've done nine round-trips so far."

"*Nine?*"

"Nine. But it isn't so bad. We've all done a lot more miles fishing out of Marblehead. Still, I signed up to shoot redcoats, not to row."

As the soldiers settled in around us, the sailor turned to me. "Say son, you wouldn't want to row this trip, would you?" he whispered. He nodded toward the other rowers, who were slumped wearily over their oars. "We've been working for hours. First it was cannon and equipment, then horses and cattle, then the reserves, and finally all of you from the front lines. You could spell a few of us. This is probably one of the last trips, anyway."

After three days on the edge of war, I was ready for the

safety of the city, and I didn't want to think about water. So I couldn't believe the words that came out of my mouth: "All right."

Immediately I regretted my decision. What if the fog lifted? What if the British ships attacked upriver while I was rowing? They'd blow us to smithereens. This might be my only chance to get away! Sometimes I could be so stupid. But before I could change my mind, the sailor stood up, stretched, and reached out for my musket.

"Son, I'll watch your gun for you. If the redcoats come, I'll need it. With this fog, though, I don't think we'll be seeing them anytime soon." He looked back at the other Marbleheaders. "Boys, my friend here is a fisherman from New London and he's going to row the next trip."

A few of the sailors grumbled, and one muttered, "You got any friends, boy?" The other sailors smiled, and with that we pushed off.

As I pulled back on the oar, I was shocked at the immense weight — this was not David and Ezra in the little rowboat! Weighed down with so many men, the rim of the boat was barely three inches from the water.

I stared at the dark water, so close to my face. Fear gripped my gut, and I forgot to row. A gruff voice from behind snapped me back to reality. "Boy, we need every oar. If you're going to do this, then do it."

As we moved out into the river, I found the rhythm of

Chapter 11

I was bone tired when our longboat pulled up to one of the wharfs in New York. I said goodbye to the Marblehead men and began trudging in the direction of where I thought I'd left David and Ezra. Exhausted soldiers were sprawled everywhere, sleeping in the morning sun. After I'd ambled around for a while, I knew my memory wasn't working too well — I wasn't getting anywhere. I asked around and finally found a man who said he'd seen the water machine.

the other rowers. We moved slowly and steadily, fog wafting about us. The water was smooth as glass. All was silent, even the oars as they entered into the water. As I angled my oar back for a pull, I saw why: the end of each oar had been wrapped with cloth to muffle sound. It was another trick to hide our evacuation from the British.

All around us heavily laden boats labored across the water. Most carried men, and a few contained the last horses to be evacuated. My arms began to burn from the rowing. I wondered how the men from Marblehead could have already rowed this same trip so many times.

To keep from looking at the water, I stared at the exhausted soldier slumped in front of me. Something about him reminded me of Papa. I think it was the weary, hopeless look in the soldier's eyes. Papa looked the same way after Mama died.

I heaved on the oar. I couldn't remember ever thinking before about how Mama's dying made him feel. I'd always thought about how it made *me* feel. Maybe Papa's feelings about me weren't just about my water fears. Maybe he was just sad and he was taking it out on me.

I wondered if Papa was even alive. A lot of men had died in the fight. Maybe he'd been wounded and was over in New York somewhere. Or maybe, just maybe, he was on one of the boats around us — even now?

Out of the corner of my eye I glimpsed another longboat pulling abreast of us, not fifty feet away. *Maybe Papa was on it!* I forced my eyes to look across the water at the boat pushing past us. Was Papa on board? I locked eyes with the first thing I saw. A large pair of bored black pupils gazed back at me and blinked.

It was a horse. I cracked a little smile at my silliness. I'd see Papa when I'd see him, I decided. Maybe in New York, maybe back in New London. Or if he'd died, I'd see him in heaven. I couldn't spend any more time worrying. I had a job to do.

The longboat was nearing New York. Once I was done rowing, I decided I'd go back and find David and Ezra. Maybe I could help with the *Turtle*. I hadn't officially signed any papers for the army, so it wasn't like I'd be deserting.

*   *   *

We dropped off the load of men in New York and pushed off to return to Long Island. Without the load of soldiers, the boat seemed to glide effortlessly across the river. I pulled my oar with ease, powering the boat with the other men across the smooth water. As we rowed in unison, I felt as though we were one mighty man on a mission. The sailor behind me whispered, "Boy, I had my doubts when that rascal Williams pulled you in, but you're all right. You're a natural sailor."

A sailor. I savored the words as we ra[ ] Brooklyn ferry. Could it really be true? [ ] sailor? A sailor who *rowed well*? A sliver [ ] inside me.

The Brooklyn ferry was empty except fo[ ] anxious soldiers and officers. Most of these s[ ] our boat. As we pushed off, another boat [ ] "They'll be the last load," whispered the sailor[ ] "Unbelievable. We got it all: men, cannon, ho[ ] ment."

In a few minutes we were several hundred y[ ] the ferry. Through the thinning fog I saw a blue [ ] up and help a tall, erect figure into the last boat. "[ ] off," said the sailor. "That would be General [ ] ton."

As we crossed the river the fog steadily lifted. S[ ] sun burst through, and the river and our boats lay e[ ] for all to see. On the distant shore tiny red [ ] appeared. A puff of smoke rose, and the thud of a c[ ] echoed across the water. The cannonball plopped [ ] lessly into the water far behind the General's boat.

Hallelujah, I thought. *The army lives.*

"Strangest thing I ever saw," he said, staring at me like I was strange for asking about it.

I found David slumped under a tree, near the battery of cannon. Tethered to the dock nearby was the *Turtle*. In the distance I saw the threatening silhouettes of British warships.

David looked up when I called his name. His eyes were sunken with fatigue and sadness.

"What's the matter?" I asked.

"Ezra's sick."

"What?" I exclaimed. "With what?"

"Camp fever," David said. "He went down after you left. Lots of soldiers have it."

I stood there stunned, absorbing the news.

"Did you find your father?" David asked.

"Naw, but I saw Butch Hyde and the battle."

David's eyes widened, and he shook his head. "I knew I shouldn't have let you go."

"What about the *Turtle?*" I asked. "Who's going to pilot it?"

Despondent, David stared at the ground. "I guess I will. I'm the only other person who knows how to operate it."

"David, you know how hard it was when you tested it in the river. You almost suffocated. It took you days to recover."

David shrugged. "What do you want me to do? Waste two years of work?" He held up his right hand, thumb and forefinger an inch apart. "I'm this close. *This close!* I'm not going to quit now. I can't."

"Ezra might get well if we just wait."

"Not with the fever. It takes you down for months." He gestured to the far-off warships. "All those targets will be gone by then. The war might be over."

I felt sorry for David. He looked pale, frail, and frustrated. Then I did what I was getting really good at: I opened my big mouth. "I'll take the *Turtle* out."

"That's nice of you, Nate, but I can't let you. For crying out loud, you're fourteen."

"On Poverty Island, I used to get in and practice. I know it all — the rudder, the oars, the intake valve, the pumps, the depth gauge, everything. Except the bomb, of course."

I stopped for a moment, reflecting on my recent actions. "David, in the last week I've been in a battle, even though I never could stand up to Butch back home. I'm scared of water, but I helped row soldiers across the river. I think I can handle a little old submarine."

David laughed. "You're a different boy than the one I recruited to help three months ago." His face got serious. "Nate, it's one thing to do a dry run on dry ground. It's an entirely different matter to paddle across a harbor with tricky currents, sneak up on a sixty-four-gun warship without being seen, submerge, and attach a one-hundred-fifty-pound bomb in complete darkness, then paddle all the way back. Think about it."

"Sixty-four-gun?" I asked. "So you've picked a target?"

"It's a secret, so don't go blabbing. There might be spies around. The redcoats have been whipping us bad, so General Putnam wants to do something dramatic. He wants me to go after Admiral Howe's flagship, the *Eagle*."

"Black Dick? We're supposed to blow up Black Dick's boat?"

"Yes, Admiral Howe himself."

"Wow!" I couldn't believe it. The little old *Turtle* — our *Turtle!* — taking on Black Dick and the top ship in the British navy. It was too good to be true.

David didn't share my enthusiasm. He stayed slumped against the tree.

"David, look at you: you're worn out," I said. "You look like a ghost."

He sighed. "I feel like a ghost."

"If you take the *Turtle* out, the currents will sweep you out to sea. You'll die out in the ocean all by yourself."

"I could think of worse ways to die."

"I can, too. You'll be too tired to row back, and the redcoats will take you prisoner. You'll rot to death in some awful prison."

"That would be worse than floating out to sea, but I'd die fast in prison since I'm so sickly."

I should have known that David wasn't afraid to die. I thought for a minute, then said, "I know why you've got to let me do it, David. You'll be too tired to row back, and the redcoats will take you prisoner, and they'll capture the *Turtle* and turn it against the Continentals."

That got his attention. His gray eyes flickered with the fire I'd seen so many times. I knew he was imagining the British blowing up Continental ships with his beloved invention. A few moments later he sighed and the glow in his eyes faded.

"Nate, I'm sorry. I'm not sending you out to get killed. This is a high-risk mission. I couldn't live with myself if something happened to you."

We sat watching the *Turtle* gently bob in the waves. "David, remember when we were first looking at the plans for the *Turtle* with Uncle Elias and Aunt Sarah?"

"Yes."

"Do you remember telling Uncle Elias that inventing is what you could do for the Revolution?"

"Yes."

"And afterward, what we talked about in the barn? You said if I helped you build the submarine, you'd help me learn to be brave?"

David frowned.

"Well, I helped you build the submarine," I said, pointing at the *Turtle*. "There it is. You did it, David, you did it!

You've done something no one else has ever done. Now your job is done. You know you're not strong enough to take the *Turtle* out. Here's your chance to help me learn to be brave. Let me pilot the *Turtle*, David. This is what *I* can do for the Revolution."

David held his head in his hands. "All right," he finally said. "I know you're up to it. I've seen you row. You know how the *Turtle* works . . . and I'm a man of my word. A deal is a deal."

"So when do we launch?"

"Tonight. The water is calm and the ebb tides should be favorable. And at least in the dark General Putnam won't be able to see how old you are." David stood up. "Try to get some rest."

I went into David's nearby tent and lay down. It was early September and the afternoon air was growing steadily colder. The enormity of what I had volunteered for was starting to sink in. I was going to single-handedly try to sink a huge enemy warship. To distract myself, I began rehearsing the operating instructions for the *Turtle*. "Push the intake valve down," I murmured. "Begin to submerge. Operate upper hand crank to move down. Maneuver under the warship. Push the screw through the tube and begin turning into the wood. Once screw is firmly in place, detach bomb. Release timer mechanism. . . ."

The next thing I knew, David was nudging me awake with his foot. "It's time, Nate."

It was dark, and the air was cool. We walked the short distance to the dock where a small group of men stood. Nearby was a whaleboat filled with sailors. The *Turtle* was tied to the boat.

"Stand tall and act old," David whispered.

"General Putnam, this is Private Wade of the Seventh Connecticut. He is highly trained with the water machine. He will be making the attack."

"I thought you were going to do it, Mister Bushnell," General Putnam said.

"Judging from the currents tonight, General, I felt it wiser to use a stronger man. It will take a lot of work to paddle out to the British fleet."

"Very well," General Putnam said. "I must confess I have a rather limited knowledge of what is involved with water machines." He turned toward me. "We're all behind you, Private Wade. Do your best. Be sure to steer clear of the enemy fort on Governor's Island."

"Yes sir," I said in my best low and husky voice.

As I lowered myself into the whaleboat, David leaned down and whispered, "I'd tell you to be careful, but if you're too careful you'll make a mistake, Nate. For this to work, you're going to have to make your fear work for you. Trust the *Turtle*. Trust yourself. You can do it."

The men rowed quietly. I longed for someone to talk to, but knew we needed to be absolutely silent. In the distance the warships loomed ominously. *Why did Ezra have to get sick?* If he'd just stayed well a few more days, I wouldn't have to be doing this!

When we were halfway to Staten Island, the rowers brought the boat to a stop. "This is as close as we dare go," one of them whispered.

I stood as the sailors pulled the *Turtle* close to the boat. I climbed up the familiar round side of the submarine and eased myself into the interior. Brass valves glittered in the moonlight. I sat on the support beam, and watched the sailors untie the ropes.

"We're casting off, son," said the sailor, and the boat slowly drew away. "Good luck." With trembling hands I pulled the hatch shut over my head. I was on my own.

In the darkness I saw a faint glow on the compass and depth gauge. I remembered the day I'd discovered the foxfire in the woods. It seemed like years ago.

With my foot I felt for the ballast intake valve. When I'd found it, I pushed down, and water gurgled into the chamber beneath me. Slowly, the *Turtle* began to submerge. *My God, what if the ballast pumps break, and I can't float back up?* A sudden panic seized me. With my hand I pushed the ballast pumps, forcing water out of the ballast tank. The *Turtle* began to rise. *Of course it works,* I thought. *Trust the* Turtle. *It's going to work.*

I pushed the ballast intake valve again. When the windows were just inches above the water line, I closed the valve. Only the conning tower was above the surface of the water. The redcoats would be darn lucky to spot such a tiny target.

So far, so good. I maneuvered the rudder until the compass showed I was pointed due west, where the *Eagle* was anchored. I inhaled deeply and felt cool air from above. The fresh air ventilators were working. I began turning the hand crank. It was slow going at first, but soon I got a rhythm going, just like rowing. Away I went into the night.

Through the windows, the vast canopy of the heavens spread out above me. Ten thousand stars glittered. The broad, dark waters of the huge harbor surrounded me for as far as I could see. In the midst of this immensity the *Turtle* and I churned along, a little round bullet headed for the heart of the British navy.

There I was, cranking along all alone in the middle of the night in a water machine. Part of me wished the *Turtle* didn't have to be a secret. There would be no guns, no marching bands, no glory. I really wished Rachel Pratt could see me. Then I thought about what she was doing back home, how she was dealing with her father. What if the rest of Saybrook had run the Pratts out of town because Mr. Pratt was a Tory? Would I ever see Rachel again?

One hour passed, then another. I churned on. Slowly but surely the British warships grew larger. There were dozens of them. Silhouetted in yellow lantern light, the rigging of the ships looked like giant cobwebs. I held my breath as the *Turtle* prowled past the first vessel. All was silent except for the slight whir of the hand crank. I knew they couldn't hear anything — the *Turtle* was underwater, after all — but I was cautious anyway. I was deep in enemy territory, and dead if some sailor spied me.

Suddenly the *Eagle* rose in front of me. The bow of the huge warship was adorned with row upon row of windows. The masts soared upwards like the tall, regal pines back home. It was the most beautiful boat I'd ever seen — and I was going to try to blow it up.

I eased the *Turtle* alongside. My arms felt like lead, but my brain was swirling. *What was I supposed to do next?* I was so scared I could barely think. With shaking hands I opened the hatch. Chilly air washed over my sweaty face, and I greedily gulped it in.

The *Eagle* towered over the *Turtle*. I could hear sailors talking far above. It was the closest I'd ever been to the enemy, except for Mr. Pratt, of course. Their strange British accents floated down. The sailors sounded young, and I wondered what they were talking about. The war? Their girlfriends back in England? What they'd had for dinner?

Strange, I'd never thought about hurting anyone when I started helping David.

I shook away the thought. What was I supposed to do next? Submerge the submarine and get under the *Eagle*. I pulled the hatch down and sat. My heart was pounding and my right leg was twitching wildly. "Leg, what is wrong with you?" I hissed. In exasperation I grabbed it with both hands and forced it down on the ballast intake valve. In a moment I was descending into the inky darkness.

Down I dropped, fast, much faster than I'd anticipated. In fact, the *Turtle* was sinking like a rock! I panicked and frantically clawed the wooden walls. I had to get out! I had to get out! If I didn't, the *Turtle* would get stuck in the mud at the bottom of the harbor — and I'd die.

Suddenly I was five again. I was falling into the river. I couldn't breathe. I could feel myself going down, flailing my arms like crazy. Then I saw a surge of bubbles above me and a flurry of arms and legs. A large figure appeared, grabbed a fistful of my hair, and yanked me upward. I relaxed and let David rescue me, and soon I was safe at the surface.

There were no bubbles this time, no rescuing hand appearing out of the dark. Instead, David's words surged up inside me. *Let your fear work for you. Trust the* Turtle. *Trust yourself. You can do it.*

I eased off the intake valve, reached over to the ballast pumps and began pumping water out. Then I reached up and began cranking the upper oars. The *Turtle* stopped sinking, hung motionless for a moment, then began to rise. *How long had I been underwater,* I wondered. *How much air was left? Did I still have time to attach the bomb?*

The *Turtle* suddenly jolted to a stop, nearly knocking me off the seat. I must have collided with the bottom of the *Eagle!* With a few thumps, I settled to a stop. *What now?* I wondered. Why, attach the bomb, of course. I remembered the wood screw attached to the top of the *Turtle.* I groped above my head and grasped an iron rod. Breathing the stale air, I strained to remember how the bomb worked. The rod was attached to an iron tube that slid up and down. The screw was attached to the top of the tube. I was supposed to push the tube and screw into the belly of the *Eagle* and twist it in. Then what? I needed to hurry, but I also needed to think.

The rod and tube detached from the screw once it was drilled into the boat. A rope ran from the screw to the bomb attached behind the *Turtle.* I felt in the dark behind me and grasped another rod. It was attached to another screw. This one released the bomb into the water and at the same time started the clock mechanism that would explode the gunpowder in exactly an hour. The rope would keep the bomb tied to the bottom of the boat.

Time to drill. I pushed the tube up and began feeling for the wood above me with the end of the screw. I felt a scrape and heard a faint metallic sound. *Strange,* I thought. I pushed the tube hard and began cranking the rod, but instead of penetrating wood the *Turtle* bounced away. When it had resettled against the bottom of the *Eagle,* I tried again. It bounced away again, as if pushed by an unseen hand. I tried five more times with the same results. Something was wrong! The razor-sharp screw should have cut right into the wood. Or maybe it *wasn't* wood. Was I hitting something else?

I was panting, and my head felt light. The air was dangerously low. I decided to surface, refresh the air, and try again. I gave the hand crank a few turns, and to my amazement, blasted out of the water like a piece of cork.

I hurriedly opened the hatch and looked upward to see if any sailors had heard the splash. All was quiet. Relieved, I closed my eyes and drank the cold, delicious air like it was buttermilk. When I looked up I noticed the ship's rigging in great detail. How strange I hadn't noticed this earlier. Were there more lanterns than before? With a shock I realized the soft light bathing the boat was the first light of dawn. Before long the *Turtle* would be exposed for the whole harbor to see. The sailors would sound the alarm, and I would be captured — or worse.

I had to think fast. I could submerge and try to attach the bomb again. Maybe I'd find wood in a different part of the boat. But by the time I resurfaced the sun would be up. I knew I'd better make a run for it while it was still dark. But then the mission would be a failure. I didn't have much of a choice. I closed the hatch, maneuvered the *Turtle* toward the east, and began working the hand crank.

I was headed back to the Battery with the worst imaginable cargo: an unexploded bomb.

Chapter 12

I groaned when I glimpsed Governor's Island on my right. I'd forgotten all about the big, fat British fort on the island. How would I get by without being seen? Something was wrong with the compass, so I couldn't submerge. I had to keep the conning tower above water so I could steer toward the Battery and not British-held Long Island.

I'd made good time, but not good enough. The sun was a growing, golden presence on the horizon, and light sped across the sky. To my horror I saw dozens of heads appear on the ramparts of the fort. Soldiers were shouting and pointing at the *Turtle*. Then a group of them scrambled down to the shore and clambered into a boat. They were coming after me!

I tried to turn the hand crank faster, but my weary arms wouldn't obey. The heavy *Turtle* was about as fast as a turtle on land. It was no match for the six redcoats bearing down on me. I looked around wildly for something to throw overboard to lighten the submarine. Everything — the valves, the cranks and rods — was permanently attached. Everything . . . except the bomb. I opened the hatch and untied the rope that ran from the screw to the bomb.

"It's a bloody rebel!" I heard one of the soldiers shout. "Faster, men!"

I dove back into the *Turtle,* pulled the hatch down, and yanked out the screw holding the bomb in place. I turned the hand crank furiously. As the *Turtle* lunged forward I looked behind me. The bomb had popped to the surface in the path of my pursuers. The timer was set for an hour, so it wasn't going to explode anytime soon. But maybe, I hoped, they would pick it up and take it back to the fort.

The soldiers stopped about fifteen feet from the mine, craning their necks as they tried to figure out what it was. "Pick it up, pick it up," I murmured. But the longboat turned, and with a flourish of oars fled back toward the island, leaving the bomb bobbing in the waves.

I forged ahead, trying to put as much distance as I could between the bomb and the *Turtle*. Ahead was the Battery with a small group of people waiting. I sighed in exhausted relief. I screwed open the hatch and waved. A few minutes later a boat was towing me in.

I leaned back and closed my eyes. My arms and shoulders burned, and my lips were dry and cracked. I wondered if this was all real. Had I really just attacked Black Dick's ship? Rowed across the harbor and back? Released the bomb? I lost track of time.

A voice broke into my misty awareness. "What happened, Nate, what happened?" I saw David's anxious face framed by the hatch. "We kept waiting to hear an explosion and nothing happened. Where's the bomb?" Too tired to talk, I just pointed to the harbor.

Suddenly two strong arms hoisted me out of the submarine. I looked up.

"Papa!" I gasped, collapsing to my knees. "What are you doing here?"

A dipper of cold water appeared before my face. I drank it and then another and another. Wiping my mouth, I looked up at the ring of concerned faces: David, General Putnam and his staff, and Papa.

"Butch Hyde told me he saw you over on the Heights," Papa said. "He said you were working on the water machine with David. I thought he was crazy, but I searched for you and David anyway."

Papa nodded toward the *Turtle.* "I guess he wasn't."

"What happened, Private Wade?" General Putnam asked. Papa looked at me and his mouth formed the word *Private?*

I smiled shyly and shrugged. "Well, I'm not sure, General. I submerged near the bow and tried and tried, but I couldn't get the screw in. I must have been doing something wrong."

David frowned. "It should have worked," he said, obviously frustrated.

"Maybe he hit copper sheathing," said the General. "A lot of their boats are using it. Makes 'em faster."

"But I — " David started. Then he looked down at the bomb-less *Turtle.* "Nate, if you couldn't attach the bomb, then . . ."

A massive explosion suddenly ripped the air. The wharf shook. An enormous column of water rose out in the harbor. We stood staring, astonished. Soldiers and civilians from the city rushed down to the waterside. "Is there an attack?" shouted one man. "Is the world ending?" cried an anxious woman.

"That'll do it for 'em!" cried General Putnam, punching his fist in the air. He was smiling the biggest smile I'd ever seen.

"So that's what you did with the bomb," David said.

"They were about to catch me," I said.

"I know. We were watching you through a spyglass. I was wondering why they gave up chase," David said. "Smart idea."

Papa was pointing to the harbor. "Look, they're leaving," he said. On the ships clustered near Staten Island, sailors were scrambling to cut cables and hoist sails. Soon, dozens of the warships were sailing across the harbor for safety!

"By God, you've made 'em run, young man!" General Putnam shouted. "The water machine from Connecticut has put the redcoats on the run!"

David turned toward me. "Didn't I tell you, Nate? Didn't I say you'd do it?"

"Well, I didn't really do it. I didn't get the *Eagle* or Black Dick. I must have done something wrong."

"I doubt it. That screw would have penetrated copper sheathing. I tested it. You know me, I leave nothing to chance." He shrugged. "Maybe it hit the metal rod that runs from the rudder. Who knows?"

David gestured toward the fleeing warships. "It doesn't really matter today. Just look, Nate. The biggest naval expedition in history is retreating from our *Turtle*." He laughed and shook his head. "You're a hero, Nate. And a brave one at that."

I laughed. *A hero?* I thought. *Brave?* It was too good to be true. But it *was* true in a way. It was like Joe Martin had said back before the battle. Courage didn't mean you never felt afraid. Courage was doing your duty even when you felt scared to death.

"And we can always try again, Nate," David said excitedly. "All we need is a new bomb and a new target."

Papa had been listening. "David, I think Nathan has proved his mettle," he said. "He's a sailor, all right; I've seen that for myself with him in this *Turtle* contraption. But he's only fourteen. He had a close call today, and I don't want him dead before his time. I'm sorry, but you're going to have to get someone else."

"But Papa," I protested. "David needs me. Ezra might be sick for a long time."

"Nathan, it's time for you to go home, and you know it. David will find someone else."

I didn't like Papa's words. But I sensed he was right, so I shut up. I'd done what I came to do. But the war was just getting started. How could I help the Revolution from Saybrook?

It was like David read my mind. He leaned close and whispered, "You can be a hero at home, too, Nate. I hear everyone is on to Mr. Pratt and his Tory ways." He winked at me. "And Rachel is going to need a brave man to help her get by."

I nodded my head slowly, trying to get my mind around this new idea. *Maybe there are many ways to be brave.* Maybe one of them was doing your duty at home when everyone else was off at war.

Of course, it didn't hurt that Rachel was the prettiest girl in town. That sure made the thought of going home easier. Heck, maybe she was watching from her window even now.

Watching for the return of the Wolf.

Epilogue

Helping Uncle Elias and Aunt Sarah on the farm wasn't as bad as I thought it would be. Ezra returned home after he had recovered, and we spent our days in the field reliving our adventure. Whenever I could, of course, I went into town to see Rachel, who was holding up pretty well. She took some heat about her father being a Tory, but I saw to it that she wasn't tarred and feathered.

The war seemed to go on forever. I can't count the number of times it seemed like the British had the Continentals licked, but somehow General Washington kept the army alive and kicking. He finally holed up the British army at Yorktown down in Virginia in 1781, and the British surrendered.

Papa came back a little later, limping from a musket ball he took at the Battle of Monmouth, but happy to be home. We all returned to New London, and I began helping Papa with the fishing business. I won't lie and say I wasn't scared the first time back on the water, but somehow it didn't paralyze me like it used to. And soon enough, the sea was like an old friend. We made a good crew, Papa and I, and sometimes we caught so many fish the other crews stared in astonishment. When I wasn't on the water, I was back in Saybrook, courting Rachel. We go for long walks, just talking, and sometimes picnic by the river. Being with her makes me so happy I could howl like a wolf.

David launched the *Turtle* against the British twice more. The submarine worked just fine, but something always kept the pilot from getting close enough to attach the bomb. Then we got word that the British shot the sloop carrying the *Turtle,* and it had sunk to the bottom of the Hudson River. We thought it was gone forever, but soon there were rumors that David had rescued his beloved submarine, and I didn't doubt it. Then the *Turtle* did disappear for good. Knowing David, I bet he dismantled his own invention so the British could never capture it and use the *Turtle* against the Colonies.

David disappeared, too, after the war. He returned to Saybrook for a while, then he left on a long trip and never came back.

Sometimes when Papa and I are out on the Sound, a big fish will break water, and for a second I see David and the *Turtle* coming up for air. Surrounded by the sea that used to scare me, I think about my freedom from fear, my own war of independence. And I thank my cousin David.

How Did the *American Turtle* Actually Work?

Please refer to the diagram on the facing page.

The pilot of the *Turtle* submerged the vessel by opening the **ballast intake** (1) with his foot, which allowed water into the **ballast tanks** (2). Once underwater, he moved the *Turtle* up and down by turning the **vertical oars** (3). The **horizontal oars** (4) in the front of the *Turtle* moved the vessel forward and backward, and the **rudder** (5) moved it left and right. To surface, the pilot cranked two hand-operated **ballast pumps** (6) to force the water out. When the vessel was above water, two **breathing tubes** (7) allowed fresh air in, and valves in the tubes automatically closed when the *Turtle* submerged.

The **depth gauge** (8) was an eighteen-inch-long glass tube, screwed into a brass pipe that allowed outside water to flow into the tube. As the *Turtle* descended, a cork inside the glass tube rose, indicating how deep the *Turtle* was underwater.

A rope connected the **wood screw** (9) to a **waterproof shell** (10), which contained a **bomb** (11). To attach the bomb, the pilot pushed the wood screw into the target, then pulled out the screw that attached the bomb to the *Turtle*. Releasing the bomb set off a **clockwork timer** (12), which ticked for an hour before it clicked on a piece of flint and created an explosion.

Diagram of the *American Turtle*

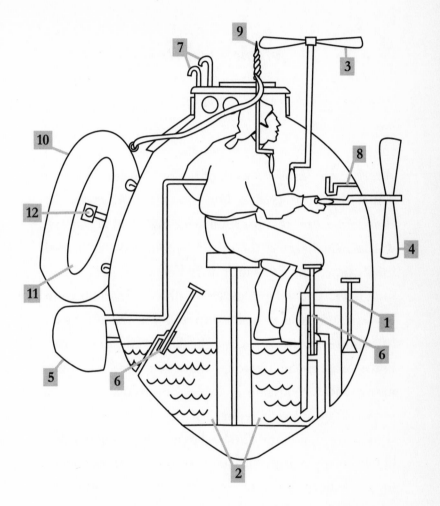

This diagram is based on an 1875 drawing by Lieutenant F. M. Barber.
Changes and corrections have been made to the original
to reflect updated research.

Author's Note

Attack of the Turtle is a work of fiction, but it is based on actual historical events. On September 6, 1776, the *American Turtle,* the first submarine ever used in warfare, was launched against the British. An engineering marvel for its time, the *Turtle* included screw propellers, a conning tower, and a depth gauge — all features still used in modern submarines. At the Intrepid Sea, Air and Space Museum in New York City, the U.S. Navy Submarine Force Museum in Groton, Conneticut, and the Connecticut River Museum in Essex, Connecticut, you can see working full-scale replicas of the *Turtle.*

The creation of the *Turtle* is fascinating in and of itself, but the many remarkable characters and events surrounding the submarine's birth make the story all the richer.

David Bushnell and his brother Ezra were real people, and David did actually design and build the *Turtle.* Nathan Wade, Butch Hyde, Rachel Pratt, Mr. Pratt, and

Josh Laribee are fictional characters, but many of their actions were based on historical events. For example, a Tory postmaster actually did intercept a letter from a friend of David's to Benjamin Franklin about the *Turtle*. The postmaster relayed the information to the British, who, fortunately for David and Ezra, never acted on it.

The actions of the famous historical figures in this book are also based on historical records. General George Washington, eager for help against the vastly superior British navy, personally approved the submarine project and gave funds to speed its development. General Israel Putnam of Connecticut, one of the heroes of the Battle of Bunker Hill, was another enthusiastic supporter of the *Turtle*. And, according to some accounts, the famous inventor Benjamin Franklin visited Saybrook and did witness the *Turtle* make a practice run. Although it is not known whether Franklin helped solve the problem of lighting the interior of the *Turtle,* it is a fact that he was the first scientist to theorize that the flashes of light often seen in the sea were produced by masses of tiny sea creatures, which he called "animalcules." Biologists have since determined those sparks are caused by microscopic organisms called dinoflagellates.

The main plot of my story is historically accurate, though I had to fictionalize some events to further the storyline. The Battle of Long Island, which was the largest land battle of the Revolutionary War, occurred one week before the launch of the *Turtle.* To recreate a scene from the battle, I drew background material from *The Revolutionary War Adventures of Joseph Martin,* the best firsthand account of the war by a Colonial soldier. Fifteen-year-old Joseph witnessed the Continental Army's frantic retreat across Gowanus Creek in Brooklyn. In a heroic rear guard action, Lord Stirling and 250 Maryland militiamen held off thousands of British and Hessian troops, buying precious time for the Continental Army to escape. All but nine of Stirling's men were killed, wounded, or captured in the savage fight. Watching from Brooklyn Heights, General Washington is said to have shouted in anguish, "Good God, what brave fellows I must this day lose!"

The evacuation of Washington's army across the East River to New York City on the night of August 29, 1776, is considered by many historians to be one of the greatest military evacuations of all time. Several regiments of Massachusetts fishermen rowed the entire 9,000-man force — along with all of the army's horses, cattle, cannon, and equipment — across the one-mile stretch of water without being detected by the nearby British.

However, the evacuation was far from complete when the rising sun threatened to unmask the Continentals' daring escape. Many soldiers recorded in their diaries accounts of a thick fog that miraculously appeared as the sun rose, cloaking the retreat for several more hours, until the last boat had escaped. According to one well-known account, General Washington, who was known to be calm in a crisis, was indeed the last man to leave Long Island.

David's brother Ezra, who was an expert at piloting the *Turtle,* did actually become severely ill shortly before the launch. At this point in the story I departed from historical accounts of the *Turtle's* first voyage and inserted Nathan Wade as the pilot. In reality, Sergeant Ezra Lee of Old Lyme, Connecticut, was hastily recruited and trained to take Ezra's place.

The details of the *Turtle's* mission are historically accurate, including the failure to attach the bomb to the *Eagle,* the explosion of the bomb to distract the pursuing British, and the panicked withdrawal of the British fleet.

No one is certain why the bomb didn't attach to the *Eagle.* David later wrote that he thought the iron bar connecting the rudder hinge with the stern was the culprit. If Sergeant Lee had simply moved a few inches, wrote David, he would have been able to attach the bomb. Another theory is that Lee became disoriented from a lack of oxygen while submerged in the *Turtle* and failed to operate the screw properly. Others think the copper sheathing that covered the bottom of many ships of that era prevented the screw from penetrating. David apparently had anticipated such a problem and ensured that the screw could drill through copper, but Lee may not have been able to apply enough pressure while underwater to penetrate copper.

Historical records indicate that the *Turtle* made two subsequent attempts to attack British ships, but vigilant sentries and the area's tricky currents foiled both efforts. A short time later, a sloop transporting the *Turtle* sank after being hit by British fire. David Bushnell did somehow retrieve the submarine, but no record exists of what happened to the *Turtle* after that. It may have been dismantled to keep the British from capturing it, or it may be at the bottom of a river near New York City. We will probably never know.

David Bushnell's inventions, however, did not end with the *Turtle*. In 1777, he developed a floating mine that destroyed a small British ship when a curious sailor hauled it onboard. Later that year, David set more than twenty underwater mines tied to buoys that looked like kegs on the Delaware River to strike British ships anchored outside Philadelphia. When one of the kegs exploded, the panicked British blazed away with cannon at the remaining kegs floating around the river, inspiring a wildly popular ballad called "The Battle of the Kegs." This song poked fun at the ferocity of the British attack on a bunch of barrels.

David eventually became a captain with the Continental Army's engineering corps, the Sappers and Miners, and served until the army was disbanded in 1783. After the war,

David mysteriously disappeared, and for forty years no one knew what became of him. The will of an 86-year-old man from Georgia finally revealed the truth. David Bushnell had changed his named to David Bush, moved to Georgia, and become a doctor. No one knows why David chose to live out his days in obscurity. Despite his effort to disappear, David's role as "the father of the submarine," as many have called him, ensures he will always hold a place in the annals of American history.

Bibliography

Commager, Henry Steele and Morris, Richard B., editors. *The Spirit of 'Seventy-six: The Story of the American Revolution as Told by Participants.* New York, New York: Harper & Row, 1975.

Gallagher, John J. *The Battle of Brooklyn, 1776.* Edison, New Jersey: Castle Books, 2002.

Gardiner, Robert, editor. *Navies and the American Revolution, 1775–1783.* Annapolis, Maryland: Naval Institute Press, 1996.

Kelly, C. Brian. *Best Little Stories from the American Revolution.* Nashville, Tennessee: Cumberland House Publishing, 1999.

Lancaster, Bruce, and Plumb, J. H. *The American Heritage Book of the Revolution.* New York, New York: Dell Publishing Co., Inc., 1963.

Latz, Michael and Rohr, Jim. "Glowing with the Flow: Ecology and Applications of Flow-Stimulated Bioluminescence." *OPN,* October 2005.

Marshall, Peter, and Manuel, David. *The Light and the*

Glory. Grand Rapids, Michigan: Fleming H. Revell, 1977.

Martin, Joseph Plumb. *Ordinary Courage: The Revolutionary War Adventures of Joseph Plumb Martin.* Edited by James Kirby Martin. St. James, New York: Brandywine Press, 1993.

McCullough, David. *1776.* New York, New York: Simon & Schuster, 2005.

McDowell, Bart. *The Revolutionary War.* Washington, D.C.: National Geographic Society, 1967.

Tall, Jeffrey. *Submarines & Deep-Sea Vehicles.* San Diego, California: Thunder Bay Press, 2002.

Taylor, Dale. *The Writer's Guide to Everyday Life in Colonial America, From 1607–1783.* Cincinnati, Ohio: Writer's Digest Books, 1997.

Wagner, Frederick. *Submarine Fighter of the American Revolution: The Story of David Bushnell.* New York: Dodd, Mead & Company, 1963.